Blackmail was a most useful tool...

"I wish, Lord Crewe, to spend the Season in London," Anne asserted.

The marquess choked and started coughing helplessly. "That is out of the question. I have my reputation to think of."

"I am not without my weapons of persuasion."

He studied her well-shaped form. "No, you are not," he agreed flatly. "But your charms won't work on me."

Anne cast him a fulminating glance, then cleared her throat. She knew she had him. "I have a diary that chronicles all the delicious *on-dits* of my life with your brother. If you do not help me, I will publish it."

THE PRIMROSE PATH

JEAN REECE

Harlequin Books

TORONTO • NEW YORK • LONDON
AMSTERDAM • PARIS • SYDNEY • HAMBURG
STOCKHOLM • ATHENS • TOKYO • MILAN

To my sister Zoula

Published March 1987
ISBN 0-373-32016-7

First published September 1980 by *Cameo*, a division
of Publication Enterprises, Inc., Volume 1, Number 3.

Printed in Canada

CHAPTER ONE

Do not, as some ungracious pastors do,
Show me the steep and thorny way to heaven,
Whiles, like a puff'd and reckless libertine,
Himself the primrose path of dalliance treads.

Hamlet, 1.iii.47-50

THE NAME on the visiting card had surprised her, and upon entering her drawing room, Anne paused for a moment, surveying her visitor curiously.

He was standing with his back to the fireplace, a powerfully built man with black hair and a strong face. His arched brows were dark and frowning, and under them a pair of hard gray eyes stared at Lady Severne. His lips curled. "So you're the wonderful Anne," observed Max Severne, the Marquess of Crewe, contemptuously, his eyes raking across her face and figure rudely. "You measure up well to your description, you trollop!"

Whatever words of greeting she'd been about to utter were frozen on her lips as Anne stiffened and stared at him in stunned silence. After an indignant moment she burst out sarcastically, "Only my intimates know me for that, my lord." Her eyes flashed angrily.

He gave an unpleasant smile. "Considering that my dear departed brother was your husband, I suppose he may be termed your intimate."

So it was he who had given that most insulting description of her to this insufferable lord. "He was my intimate only now and then," she snapped, not considering her words, so angry was she.

"Meaning you were busy elsewhere?"

She turned away. "Or he," she said in a stifled voice.

"Don't pitch that gammon to me, Lady Severne," Max said. "My brother may not have been all amiability, but he was certainly faithful."

His pompous tone infuriated her. "And I'm sure you're in a position to know," she said icily.

"I know that if there was any havy-cavy business going on in your marriage, you were the perpetrator, not my brother."

Anne bit her lip, quelling a sharp retort. This fellow was beyond anything she had ever encountered. She took a quivering breath and tried to subdue the demon of fury raging through her.

"Do be seated, my lord," she said in as polite a voice as she could muster, indicating a wing chair. "I will ring for tea." She hoped her good manners would put this visit upon a more pleasant footing. But she doubted it. She turned to the bellpull and had to exercise considerable restraint not to rip it from the ceiling in her anger.

"I have no intention of taking tea with you today, my lady," he said abruptly, disposing himself comfortably in the chair.

"You mean, one hopes, that you have no intention of prolonging this most unpleasant visit another moment?" she asked, her teeth gritted.

His eyes gleamed at that. "This *is* a most unpleasant visit for me, my lady. How perceptive of you."

Tilly, the housekeeper, bustled into the room, looking expectantly at her mistress.

"Please bring in some tea and cakes, Tilly." Anne directed her in a quiet voice, and the housekeeper curtsied and left.

"I told you I have no intention of taking tea with you," the marquess said.

"And I am most glad to hear it," she returned pleasantly, seating herself on the settee. "But I wished to be armed with a teapot to fling at your head, my lord, if you dare to enrage me again."

The tone in which she delivered this statement was even and calm. But Crewe couldn't have been more startled if she had screamed it.

"Again your description is confirmed," he said with grim satisfaction after a short pause. "I'd been told you were a woman of no delicacy of principles and of poor conduct."

"It's a pity no one warned me of your character, my lord," she said. "Else I would have taken the precaution of bolting the doors against you."

He smiled condescendingly. "You will be most happy you did not do so, my lady. The purport of my business with you is much in your favor."

She eyed him skeptically but vouchsafed no answer. Tilly reentered the room, puffing under the weight of the tea service. She placed the tray on the Pembroke table beside Anne.

"Thank you, Tilly. That will be all."

Under the pretext of being engrossed in pouring herself a cup of tea, Anne took the opportunity of studying her brother-in-law critically. He was what would be described as an out-and-outer, everything prime about him. This realization afforded her no pleasure, so she allowed herself the luxury of taking into dislike the snowy whiteness of his cravat, painstakingly tied in the Mathematical, the perfect set of his riding coat, which was cut so close to his form that she had no doubt he needed to be helped into it by two servants, the immaculacy of his buckskins and the superfluity of the three ridiculous tassels that dangled from the white tops of his gleaming Hessian boots. She tried not to acknowledge to herself the perfection of his figure, with its wide shoulders and fine leg, or his countenance, which, with its straight nose, firm mouth and dark gray eyes, was so handsome as to be almost startling.

The marquess endured this scrutiny with equanimity, returning the favor by studying her even more closely.

He shrugged after a moment and gave her his verdict. "Quite a pretty piece, I allow. But certainly not worth throwing away a fortune on."

"I'm sure Simon knew what he was doing when he married me," Anne replied haughtily.

"As he was caught in your toils, madam, I'm equally sure he had not the slightest control of his actions."

Anne could not help but smile at this. The idea of Simon's being caught in anyone's toils was too ludicrous for consideration. "One would almost think you didn't know your brother very well," she said after a moment.

"One would definitely think that my poor brother didn't know *you* very well when he married you, but of course he soon learned his mistake."

Anne almost retorted that the boot had been on the other leg, but she had no intention of allowing this ungracious lout a peep into her private life. "When was the last time you spoke with your brother?" she asked.

Her eyes gleamed with satisfaction as he acknowledged a hit. "Knowing that you and my brother junketed about the Continent the whole time since your most unpropitious marriage, I think you are aware that I didn't set eyes on him, let alone speak with him, after that date."

"Much can develop in a gentleman's character in four long years, my lord."

"I'm sure they were four very long years for my brother, my lady. His death could only have been a happy release for him."

Anne gripped her hands together and closed her eyes.

"The teapot is at your elbow," he reminded her helpfully.

Her eyes flew open and she almost availed herself of the handy weapon before she realized that it would afford him great pleasure to see my lady Severne behaving no better than a fishwife. "Very true," she snapped after a silent struggle with herself. With a great show of calmness, she poured herself another cup of tea.

He grinned.

"How ungentlemanly you are," she sniffed.

"How unladylike you are," he replied with aplomb.

"Considering that you never set eyes on me before today, I find your annihilation of my character slightly unconvincing."

His finely shaped mouth hardened, and his face took on a most unpleasant expression. "Considering that I acquired this reading of your character through the sporadic letters I received from Simon each time he needed money, I think it can be said that I know you very well. And being apprised of the great suffering and hardship you caused my brother, I think my description of you as unladylike highly forbearing."

"Trollop being closer to the truth," she sneered, with flashing eyes.

"And harpy even closer," he replied.

"If you believed that, my lord, why did you always send money to Simon whenever he applied for it? It must have gone much against the grain for you to support my wicked ways."

"It did. But since Simon had been disowned by my father upon his elopement with you, I felt it was the least I could do. His letters made me pity him so. What need was there for me to torture him more when he had so much to suffer from you?"

She set her cup in its saucer with a snap. Heat rushed to her face, and she seethed with indignation. A strong sense of ill-usage made her wish to burst into tears, but she was a woman of pride, and she quelled this ignoble impulse. She did not care a fig what the marquess thought of her. He was the greatest beast in nature, besides being rude and unconciliating, and if she didn't box his ears in a moment, it would not be through any fault of hers.

"I suggest we leave off talking of me. We shall soon be at loggerheads, my lord, our opinions on that subject being so very different."

"I would imagine they must be," he murmured. "But I'm afraid I cannot oblige you, for the purpose of my visit is about yourself."

"Well, don't keep me on tenterhooks, my lord. Just what is the purpose of this visit?"

"I think I shall keep you in suspense a few moments longer, just to get my own back, you see. You have no idea the time and trouble you cost me in locating you."

"It is a shame you managed to succeed."

"So very difficult," he continued, as though he had not been interrupted, "that I began to cherish the hope you had disappeared from the face of the earth. Considering that you have lived in Austria, France and Germany in your checkered career, one would have supposed that your own home in Devonshire was too tame stuff for words."

"Well, it was tame stuff until you entered it, my lord."

"One can only think that you took refuge here on a holiday before returning to your wonted existence as a high-flyer."

She took a very deep breath at this, her fists clenched. In a moment she was positive she was going to grab the poker from the fireplace and brain him with it.

"I don't wish to appear an ungracious hostess, my lord," she said after a long moment, "but perhaps you'll excuse me and allow me to leave your most ingratiating presence until you've decided you've waited long enough to tell me the reason for your visit. After whatever length of time you deem proper, you have only to ring the bell, and I shall return to you with alacrity.''

She rose from the settee and prepared to sweep from the room, but he detained her with a gesture.

"Take a damper,'' he advised her weariedly. "The purpose of my visit is to apprise you of the fact that you've become the beneficiary of quite a honey-fall.''

She stared at him blankly. "I beg your pardon?''

"Please do.''

Her eyes sparked at this, but she refused to rise to that bait, so puzzled was she at his words. "A honey-fall, you said?''

"Yes, something close to thirty thousand pounds.''

"Thirty thousand pounds,'' she echoed faintly. The matter-of-factness with which he delivered this leveler tickled her and caused her to say dramatically, "Quick, get me my hartshorn and water! I think I'm going to have a fit of the vapors.''

"Very funny, my lady,'' he snapped, not missing her twinkling eyes. "I am serious.''

"I should hope so,'' she said severely. "Wouldn't you be ashamed to raise false hopes in a poor widow's breast?''

He considered her figure dispassionately for a moment. "Not really.''

If she hadn't been so angry, she would have laughed. "You are very insensitive.''

"No, just disgusted. But that's neither here nor there. All I'm here to do is to inform you that you are now the possessor of a handsome independence.''

"Handsome?'' she ejaculated despite herself. "I'd call thirty thousand pounds a fortune.''

"You, of course, may call it anything you wish, since it is yours."

She gave him a puzzled frown not unmixed with impatience. Surely he couldn't be serious. He was doing it rather too brown as far as she was concerned. "If this is all some hoax, my lord, I would be greatly pleased if you'd leave my house this instant."

"Oh, I shall leave, and quite readily, I might add, soon enough," he said coolly. He took an enameled snuffbox from his pocket and flicked it open with one hand. He then sniffed a pinch with a delicate twist of the wrist.

Anne cast him a glance of the greatest dislike. "Just how was I so lucky as to receive this honey-fall, my lord?"

"Unfortunately, through the death of my parent."

She was silent at this, feeling for him in his bereavement but uncertain how to express her sentiments.

"Oh, spare me your condolences, please," he said sharply. "I'm sure they'd be quite as long as they'd be insincere, and I have no wish to be bored."

She folded her lips resolutely, unwilling to let his words upset or hurt her in the least. "Which parent?" she asked.

"My father, of course," he snapped. "And had he known what a heartless hussy you are, he never would have left a bequest to you."

"What, do you mean you didn't tell him what a heartless hussy I am?" she asked, her blue eyes open wide in an innocent gaze.

"Unfortunately, I did not."

"Why ever not?"

"To spare his feelings," he said shortly. "He felt badly enough about having cast his younger son into the world without a penny to his name." He almost snarled these words, and Anne blinked.

"Then why did he do it?"

"Because he felt it to be his duty, as hard as it was. He couldn't sanction such a scandal in the family as an elopement to Gretna Green. He had forbidden Simon to marry without his permission, but Simon chose to marry against him, anyway. Simon therefore had to bear the consequences. In all our long history no member of our family has ever caused a scandal."

"What a dull lot you must be," she murmured.

"No." He eyed her with hostility. "Just proper."

"That's what I meant. And you must be the dullest of them all." He looked ready to bite off her nose at that, but she stopped him with a wave of her hand. "No need to fall into the fits over Simon's predicament, however. He did have the money you gave him."

"A paltry amount, and you know it."

"Indeed I do know it."

Crewe leaned forward and fixed her with a burning glare. "That knowledge did not prevent you from encouraging Simon to throw it away on every profligacy imaginable. I see that you didn't suffer from your straitened circumstances," he sneered, indicating the pearl necklet she wore. "They must have cost Simon a pretty penny."

The pearls were the one piece of her jewelry Simon had never been able to induce her to pawn. They were not of the finest quality, but she attached a great sentimental value to them because they had been a gift to her from her mother.

"One can only infer that your knowledge of fine jewelry is rudimentary, my lord."

Crewe cracked an unpleasant laugh. "Or perhaps yours. You did pick them out, didn't you?"

"You are mistaken," she said when she could trust her voice. Her throat was tight and her face was burning. She unclenched her fists and smiled. "You know," she said with an air of studied unconcern, "Simon needed little encouragement to be profligate."

"Yes. Obviously your tiny inducements were most effective. You had him wrapped around your little finger, didn't you?"

She gave a hollow laugh. "Obviously." He was impossible. His mind was made up, and nothing she could say would change it.

He leaned back into his chair, his countenance emptied of all expression. After a moment, he shrugged. "It was obvious to me, but not to my father. He died feeling he needed to make some reparation to his son."

"So he left a fortune to his son's widow."

"He did not know you were a widow."

Anne stared at him an uncomprehending moment. "He didn't know I was a widow?"

"No."

Anne frowned, shaking her head. "He must have known. I wrote him a letter. Simon's body was sent to you."

Crewe winced at the word "body" but continued staring at her with a wooden countenance. "His body was sent to me, not to my father. I took the greatest pains to keep Simon's death a secret from him."

"But why?"

In a cool and controlled voice that revealed the suppressed violence of the emotions he was experiencing, Max said, "I did not wish him to learn that Simon had died in a scandalous duel trying to defend his wife's sullied reputation."

Anne gasped aloud, unable to credit her hearing. "Why do you say that?"

His lips curled. "You think me a greenhorn. I have my channels."

"Completely trustworthy ones, I see." She was angrier now than she could have thought possible.

"I assume none of the more succulent details of the affair were left out?" he said, a question in his dark eyes.

She opened her mouth, then closed it. She shook her head, tense. "No, you have the most palatable ones, my lord."

He nodded. "I did, but my father did not. He was invalidish at the time, and he could not have borne such a terrible scandal. It would have killed him. Thus my small discretion has left you in a very enviable position."

"Yes, I see; indeed it has." Her nostrils flared as she tried to subdue her wrath. Her eyes narrowed. "But knowing of my dreadful character, you didn't have to follow out your father's bequest."

He looked down his nose at her with repugnance. "I do have pride, madam. It would be beneath me to do anything not worthy of the Severnes."

She became very still, thinking. *Oh, it would, would it?* Suddenly she was seized by an irresistible determination to teach this insufferably straitlaced monster a lesson. Never a scandal in his family? Well, she vowed then and there to do everything in her power to embroil this Marquess of Crewe in the worst scandal possible, something he could not live down. He would pay for his insults. He been sent to her for a purpose—to be administered the set-down of which he was in such crying need. It would be her mission in life. How she would enjoy arranging it! But she needed time. She saw that his brows were raised slightly at her silence, and she forced a shrug. "I am merely speechless with surprise that you could allow a fortune to fall into the hands of an accredited adulteress and accessory to murder."

"It is difficult to bear, I admit," he said, twirling his quizzing glass. "But be assured the fortune is not going to fall instantly into your hands."

"Oh, so you have been bamming me all along!" she breathed.

"Not at all; the fortune is real, but you see, I am the trustee of that fortune."

Her hands tightened convulsively, her body suddenly rigid.

His eyes gleamed with pleasure. "That is unsettling information, isn't it?"

She closed her eyes to calm herself. She held up her hand. "Now, let me see if I have this clearly," she said. "I have been left a fortune of thirty thousand pounds by your father in an uncontested bequest. Is that correct?"

He nodded affirmatively.

"And you hold the purse strings."

Again, he nodded affirmatively.

She flung herself up from her chair, ready to tear his brother's character to shreds, and to tell this marquess to go to the devil and to take his fortune with him, but suddenly she paused. She looked down on the marquess through narrowed eyes. The fortune would come in handy in her determination to teach this fellow a lesson. She shouldn't whistle it down the wind, at least not yet. She gave a pert smile. "I daresay we shall manage to rub tolerably well together, brother."

He sat bolt upright. "I think you much mistake the matter, Lady Severne. And I would be most appreciative if you would not call me brother."

She opened her eyes wide at this. "I perceive you still don't approve of me, my lord," she observed with sorrowful irony.

"I disapprove of you heartily," he replied.

She gave a slight smile but hooded her eyes. "Dear me, how straitlaced you are. I had no idea we had a pastor in the family."

"Well, I had every idea we had an abbess," he said maliciously.

Her eyes flashed at this insult. He might as well have called her mistress of a brothel! She nodded slowly. "Yes. I can see that associating with me will be a most distasteful duty for you, my lord."

"Not nearly as distasteful as it will be for you, I assure you."

That remains to be seen, Anne thought. She held out her hand. "It was most kind of you to call, my lord. I'm sure you must realize how your surprising news has overset me. You'll be so kind as to allow me time for reflection, if you please, and call again tomorrow at your convenience. You are putting up in this district, are you not?"

He rose from his chair but declined to take her hand. She dropped it readily enough. "Indeed. I would take no chance of being put up by you, my lady. I am staying at the Red Lion."

She gave a stiff smile. "I hope it meets with your puritanical tastes, my lord."

He nodded shortly. She led him to the door.

"Don't forget to call again tomorrow," she reminded him. "We have much to discuss."

The Marquess of Crewe bowed his leave-taking, and Anne returned to the drawing room in the highest dudgeon. She flung into the room, slamming the door behind her, so that the Sèvres wall plaques rattled. She paced furiously about, finally relieving her overcharged emotions by taking up a Spode figurine and flinging it into the grate so that it shattered with a most satisfyingly explosive sound. How she wished the marquess would return to the room—only for a moment, mind—so that she could take the toasting fork and skewer him with it. She would like to flay him alive.

She sat down on the settee and conceived the most exquisite tortures to visit upon this gentleman—from tearing out his black hair to beating him with her reticule. However, after a moment's reflection, she told herself there was no need to resort to such uncivilized modes of revenge. She had already hit upon the very thing. She would ruin him. She would effect the Marquess of Crewe's total social, physical and mental downfall. Oh, he made her angry beyond all reason. He was like some damned ungracious pastor. Pastor Max. Well, he couldn't possibly be such a complete model of virtue. He must have weaknesses. And she would expose them. If only for his own good. But, she thought with satisfaction, it would really be for *her* own good.

Her machinations were interrupted by a timid tapping upon the door and the immediate admittance of Tilly into the room. The old woman eyed Anne doubtfully. Anne looked up and gave a crooked smile. "Tilly, you must congratulate me. I've just inherited a fortune."

"That's just what I was telling myself," the woman said sardonically. "What with you looking as blue as megrims, I told myself, I said, something marvelous must have happened to my mistress."

"No, I mean it. Something marvelous indeed. Not the least of which was making the acquaintance of my brother-in-law, the Marquess of Crewe, Max Severne."

Tilly nodded wisely. "Quite a natty gentleman that. Not but what he's a little high in the instep."

"He's insufferable!" Anne exclaimed, not mincing matters. "He's a starched-up stiff-rump, proud and puffed up in his own conceit."

"Just as you say, my lady. I only had a glimpse of him, mind, so I wasn't allowed such a thorough reading of his character as you was."

A little of Anne's temper abated at Tilly's words. Her brow cleared and she laughed. "How unprincipled you are to take the wind out of my eye like that."

Tilly smiled. "But what, my dear, has put you in such a taking?"

"My brother-in-law, of course," Anne informed her, sobering, her eyes glittering.

"Wasn't what you expected him to be?"

Anne twisted her hands together. "I had no expectations of him at all. But he, however, had every expectation of finding his sister-in-law a confirmed strumpet."

Tilly gasped, and Anne nodded with grim satisfaction.

"He could never have said such a thing!" Tilly protested.

"Oh, he said much worse." Anne looked up, her countenance aflame. "Please know, Tilly, that Simon died in a duel over me!"

"Stuff and nonsense," Tilly snorted.

"Not to my lord Max Severne. I'm an adulteress, you see, and Simon was my noble, long-suffering husband."

Tilly flew to the settee and put her arms about her mistress, hugging Anne's head to her shoulder. "Oh, my poor lamb. Never you mind," she soothed. "Don't you be thinking about Simon no more. He's dead and gone, thank heaven. And it's a crying shame you ever had anything to do with him, either."

Anne gave a tearful sniff and pulled her cambric handkerchief from her reticule. She heartily agreed with Tilly's sentiments but thought it unbecoming to state her opinions of her husband aloud. Tilly had no such reservations and animadverted on the gentleman's wicked character at some length. Anne couldn't have said it better. Simon *was* a blackguard, a cad, a scoundrel. Not only had he taken gross advantage of her sensibilities, when she was but just coming out of the schoolroom, by making her fall in love with him, but he had been devil enough to talk her into eloping with him, just to put his father's nose out of joint. Anne had been in love, starry-eyed, too blinded by her love to realize what a serious step it was to elope with Simon to Gretna Green. Her parents turned their backs on her. Simon was cut off from his family and his income, no longer accepted in society, so they fled to the Continent.

And there Anne began a life of misery. She had been dazzled by Simon. He was a lord's son. He was handsome and dashing, with easy address. But the luster soon wore off. In a short time she found Simon to be a selfish, dissolute and cruel monster. He became a frequenter of all the worst gaming hells in Europe and was not loath to take his young bride along as bait for gudgeons who were ripe for plucking in a card game. He was a heavy imbiber, however, often playing when his faculties were beclouded by blue ruin and brandy, and he lost heavily. He recouped his losses by cheating, fuzzing the cards. But he practiced this stratagem once too often and had to pay his dues by looking down the barrel of a dueling pistol.

"And I wish to goodness," Tilly continued, "that Lord Barrymore had appeared in the first year of your marriage instead of your fourth and sent Simon Severne to his grave that much sooner."

"No, Tilly," Anne admitted, "whatever hardships I endured in my marriage were incurred through my own folly." When she had first seen him, at a party at a friend's home, she should have run from him instead of letting herself become infatuated.

"But you was just a babe and not responsible!" Tilly exclaimed.

Anne sat up and straightened her skirts purposefully. "I know. A romantic girl. But I'm not a child now, Tilly, and I won't pine away for what is past and done with. That brother of his is not going to make me remember all those horrible years I've tried so hard to forget."

Anne had long ago tried to put that unpleasant time of her life out of her mind, deeming it the healthiest thing to do. Sometimes her thoughts reverted to a particularly hellish night when Simon came home ape-drunk and ready for a night's larking. She was far from desirous of indulging him and therefore had to endure savage reproaches and not just a few blows, but these recollections were few and far between and she resolutely banished them from her mind.

At this moment, something of far greater importance was taking up her thoughts: her encounter with the Marquess of Crewe. Again she seethed with indignation at his defamation of her character. As though he were some pattern-card of perfection himself, qualified to sit in judgment upon another human being.

She must have been scowling, for Tilly pinched her cheek and said, "Now don't be in such a pucker, dear. It will ruin your appetite, and I've had Cook prepare you such a nice meal."

IN THE EVENING Anne ate her meal without any relish, and afterward, as was her wont, she returned to the sitting room to do some needlework while Tilly read aloud to her. She usually worked until the candles guttered in their sockets. Anne had inherited her house in Devonshire after her parents' death. Thank goodness they hadn't disinherited her for marrying Simon. It was a tiny house in a pretty valley. The life she led in it was uneventful and quiet, but compared with the life she had led with her husband, it was paradisiacal indeed.

Tonight, however, she found it impossible to concentrate on her work, and finally she gave it up, determining to go up to her bedchamber, claiming a headache. Tilly did not detain her, only suggesting she burn some pastilles and drink some barley water, directions Anne promptly forgot. She did not really have a headache. She only wished for some seclusion and quiet in which to ponder the day's occurrences.

One thing was certain. She detested the Marquess of Crewe. He was a pompous lobcock. A consequential, pot-sure bacon-brain. Oh, how she wished to put him in his place!

He must be a complete noddy to believe so readily the things Simon wrote about her. Simon, of course, had simply been enlisting for Crewe's sympathy so that his brother would send him money. She toyed with the notion of revealing Simon's and her own true character. She knew quite a few individuals who would be willing to speak for her. But she dismissed this as a craven action. Besides, she thought darkly, he wouldn't credit it one bit. Not even if she showed him the diary she had kept during her sojourn on the Continent. It was filled with her unsavory experiences with Simon. She had used it as a method to vent all her frustration, hurt and anger. It did not make for pleasant reading.

She suddenly became very still. Her mind reeled as she was struck with an idea.

She wanted to trap her virtuous, complacent brother-in-law, to embroil him in some terrible scandal that would make him ashamed for the rest of his days. Well, in order to do so, she would have to live in London. He might not relish having her present herself to the polite world. He might even refuse to let her do so. But, she thought, going to the bed and reaching under her pillow and pulling out her diary, then flipping through its pages, he might be induced to allow her her wishes. The diary might be the perfect inducement.

Anne had been a girl of very lively spirits, almost to the point of mischievousness when given half a chance. Once an idea was engendered, she followed it through to its limit, wherever it led her. She absently divested herself of her muslin dress and donned a pretty dressing gown of clean, crisp cotton. She combed out her blond hair and braided it deftly. Then she climbed into bed and pulled the bedclothes up to her chin. To be sure, she had been living a most dull existence. She wondered how she had tolerated it. Going through the days, each one the same as the last, for over two years. She was an heiress now and must change her ways. She smiled as her head sank in the pillow. Or get the marquess to change his!

ANNE WAS WAITING for him the next day and was able to watch his arrival from a window. He pulled up in a perch phaeton drawn by a team of matched bays. Obviously, from the way he stopped in front of her house, he was a top-of-the-trees sawyer, able to drive to an inch, keeping his leaders well in hand. It was quite a beautiful team, matched to a hair. Must have cost him a small fortune, although she doubted he cared a rush for that.

From what Simon had told her of his elder brother, Max Severne was the heir to a vast fortune, extensive lands and a country seat that rivaled in magnificence the Duke of Marlborough's Blenheim Palace. And he was well aware of his consequence. He didn't deign to grace any circle in society but the highest, the Carlton House set. He was much admired for his taste in clothes, horses and art objects, as well as for his face, rank and fortune.

Simon had envied him only his rank and fortune, always begrudging his brother the position of being firstborn and heir. Simon would have infinitely preferred the title to fall upon his own head, but fate was perverse. Fate might be perverse, but Simon had been worse. He had willfully brought ruin on his and his wife's heads. She caught herself up at this thought and shook her head. She was a pea-goose going on in this way. She must forget the past, especially when the future looked to be so interesting.

The marquess was led into the drawing room, where Anne awaited him with a deceptive air of unconcern. At his entrance she put down a book, of which she had read not a word, and rose to give greeting.

"I see you have recovered your countenance, my lady," the marquess observed. He was in riding dress, a rig-out that became him admirably, but Anne refused to be impressed by his handsome face and inspiring height.

"I'm so glad you deemed it proper to return today, my lord. I was beginning to think you had decided not to reenter this den of iniquity."

"I daresay your eagerness for my return was not caused by my wonderful personage but by my wonderful news yesterday," he said suavely.

She smiled sweetly. "Yes, learning that one had become an heiress was wonderful news," she agreed. "But that you were willing to acknowledge my connection with your family was also wonderful."

"It was my father's willingness, not mine."

"But I am now connected with you, am I not, since you are my trustee? And my brother-in-law, remember?"

"You will not gain much joy from the connection," he said, looking indifferently at his well-pared nails.

Anne kept a prudent silence. Tilly entered with the tea tray.

"I do hope you'll partake of some tea with me today. I've had a plum cake especially baked."

"How generous of you," he said sarcastically.

"Not at all." She poured him a cup of tea and waited until he had sat down and taken a large mouthful of cake before she dropped her bombshell.

"I wish, Lord Crewe, for you to arrange matters for me to spend the Season in London."

He choked and started coughing helplessly. She schooled her countenance and stared at the ceiling.

"What did you say?" he asked in a voice of dangerous quiet.

"I wish, Lord Crewe, for you to arrange matters for me to spend the Season in London," she repeated kindly.

"That is out of the question," he said grimly.

She was undismayed. "Oh, but I'm sure it must not be. I'm now an heiress, you know. I should be quite a catch on the marriage mart, and I wish to see if I cannot cause a stir in the town."

There was a twinkle of sardonic amusement in his eyes. "I'm sure you would set the town on its ears, my lady. But I'm afraid I will not allow such an expenditure of your funds."

"Oh, but you must. I've decided I've been leading a very monotonous life here in Devonshire and feel London is the very thing to enliven it."

"But you are not the very thing for London," he said adamantly. "It is impossible. I have my reputation to think of. Let us leave it at that. Now, I have set up your inheritance in a trust, the income of which will fall to you—"

She interrupted him. "We will *not* leave it at that."

"How very mulish you are," he observed dispassionately.

She did not take exception to this unflattering description but only shrugged. "Far be it from me to point out that the same may be said of you. You are mulish and also stupid."

His eyebrows lifted disdainfully. "How may that be?"

"I am not without my weapons of persuasion, you know," she began.

He looked at the teapot significantly and shook his head. Then he looked at her well-shaped form and her face, with its sparkling blue eyes, straight nose and full lips. She was quite a beauty. Her aureole of golden hair, her lovely countenance and her graceful air all created a picture that would move any man's heart. Lord Crewe, however, was unmoved. "No, you are not," he agreed flatly. "But your charms won't work on me."

She blushed despite herself and was quite angry for doing so. She bit her lip. "That was not what I meant," she said waspishly.

"Oh, do forgive me."

She cast him a fulminating glance, then cleared her throat. She felt quite breathless, barely able to suppress an anticipatory smile of triumph. She knew she had him. "You must know, my lord, that during my connection with your brother, I kept a diary that chronicles all the most delicious *on-dits* of our life together. If you do not help me to a Season in London, I will publish my diary to acquire the monies I need."

CHAPTER TWO

MAX LOOKED AS THOUGH he'd been landed a facer.

Anne continued a little breathlessly. "I believe it would be most distasteful for you, my lord, to have your brother's doings on everyone's tongue."

"It would be his wife's doings that would cause the scandal!" he said hotly.

She put up her chin. "Well, I am connected with you, my lord, remember? I'm a Severne, too. And as you pointed out, there's never been a scandal in your family's long history." She paused. "So far."

His face took on an ugly expression. "I don't take kindly to blackmail."

"You'll get used to it."

"Unscrupulous creature. Doxy!"

She winced but bore up remarkably well. "Pigeon."

"You'll find me a poor pigeon for the plucking."

"But it's *my* money, Lord Crewe," she pointed out in justification.

He conceded her point but without much grace. He surveyed her carefully, his hand to his square chin. "This is no idle threat?"

"I have a powerful inclination to stay in London for the Season."

Her tone was devoid of any special significance, but he frowned suspiciously. "Why?"

"I might wish to find a husband."

"Or a lover!"

She nodded. "There is that possibility. But just consider, Lord Crewe. If I do remarry, I shall no longer be connected with your family."

Her words made Max sneer. "A strong inducement, obviously." He stared at her, a hard expression on his face. She returned the stare unwaveringly.

There was a long, uncomfortable silence. Anne's heart began to beat rapidly, and her mouth felt dry. He stood up stiffly, his face immobile. Her breath rushed out in a gasp of astonishment as he said, without preamble, "I take it you wish to go to the heights of society." Noting her openmouthed surprise, he lifted his eyebrows superciliously. "You expected some useless expostulation, perhaps? But I always try to behave the gentleman, you see, and I'm not one to vent my spleen before a blackmailer."

Anne was too filled with a surging sense of triumph to take exception to this epithet. She swallowed rather noisily and said as coolly as she could, "You're very sensible, my lord. And I, of course, do indeed wish to rise to the very heights."

"Then I shan't fob you off with a mere second cousin of mine but shall put you into the hands of my great-aunt, the Duchess of Byrne."

Anne was slightly taken aback. She had no desire to rub elbows with nobility, although she knew it would add greatly to her consequence to enter the ton under the aegis of a duchess.

"How considerate of you to suggest it," she murmured, her mind seething with barely suppressed excitement.

"I merely wish to take the best of care of my fair blackmailer," he replied coldly, without a change of expression. "I don't want you to take a pet and publish your diary just because you aren't pleased with my efforts."

"Oh, don't be put about because I got the better of you," she admonished. "It is highly unsportsmanlike of you."

"No doubt, but I've never before sported upon the field of human plucking."

"While I'm a practiced artist at it, I suppose," she hissed indignantly.

He nodded, a sneering smile on his lips.

She had to bite back a furious retort.

He took his beaver hat in his hand. "Don't look so affronted, my lady. You have gained your objective and should be crowing with delight."

"Well, I don't see why you should be so Friday-faced," she sniffed. "I won't be staying with you in London."

"A small consolation," he replied. "I am simply angry with myself for not having guessed how unprincipled you would be, you see. A diary, of all things!" He shook his head in disgust, then controlled himself, taking out his snuffbox and sniffing a pinch. "I can only hope, my dear lady, that London lives up to all your expectations," he said, with a slight bow.

Her expectations would surprise him. She steadied her temper by dwelling on the great pleasure she would derive in making this Pastor Max a social outcast.

He returned his snuffbox to his capacious pocket. "I shall leave now, if you do not mind. I must return to town and prepare Lady Byrne for your advent."

Doubt shook her. "Will she be thrown into a flutter?"

He considered her words a moment, an odd twinkle in his eyes. "The duchess thrown into a flutter? Why, no," he said slowly. "I'm fairly assured she will not be."

Anne sighed in relief. The duchess was probably made of resilient stuff. A regular Tartar, no doubt. She most certainly would be unbearable to live with, but Anne was willing to bear much in order to teach this Pastor Max a lesson.

Tilly led Crewe to the front door, and Anne watched at the window until the phaeton rolled away. Then she gave a loud whoop and executed a little caper. What an interesting turn her life had suddenly taken!

THE MARQUESS OF CREWE arranged for Anne's travel to London, hiring a post chaise and bespeaking job horses at various inns along the route. He sent his groom over to place himself at Anne's service, and she couldn't help but be impressed at this consideration. He had probably done it not out of consideration, though, but from sheer habit. He was used to behaving the grand lord, indulging himself in every luxury.

But Anne was certainly not used to indulging herself in every luxury. It was an unlooked-for comfort to place all the responsibilities for a trip to London on someone else's shoulders.

And it was a pleasure to be able to direct Tilly, in the airiest voice possible, to pack only the veriest necessities for a trip to London, for she had every intention of furnishing herself with a completely new wardrobe upon her arrival there.

"Well, if that don't beat all to flinders." Tilly gasped involuntarily, her eyes widening. "London, of all places!"

They did not set off for this paradise until a letter was received from the Duchess of Byrne indicating her consent for Anne's visit. The letter was written on thick vellum paper and was set with a gold seal. Most impressive.

Anne had no time to discover that the Duchess of Byrne was a lady of some consequence in the ton. She was an intimate of Queen Charlotte and had a great deal of social clout. Due, no doubt, to her title and her wealth.

Once confident of the duchess's complaisance, Anne delayed not a moment in beginning her journey.

The trip took three days, but it was not tedious in the least. The chaise was well sprung and driven at a spanking pace. No delays were incurred at tollgates, because the tiger blew his yard of tin, and they sailed right through. The changing of horses, thanks to Max's instructions, was accomplished with lightning speed. And Anne beguiled the hours by picturing in her mind the methods of Max's downfall.

Highgate, the last stage of the journey, allowed Anne and Tilly a panoramic view of the red-bricked metropolis. Anne clasped her hands tightly in excitement as the chaise made straight for Mayfair's Grosvenor Square. Within moments, the horses pulled up before a massive edifice.

Two footmen promptly descended the front steps to open the chaise door. Anne was overwhelmed for a moment and looked at Tilly, who was clutching a bandbox to her breast. Then Anne smiled and squeezed Tilly's hand. "You look as though you expect to be eaten alive," Anne said, giggling.

"I'd like to see them try," Tilly answered, pot-valiant, eyeing the approaching footmen with defiance.

Anne, however, smiled kindly at the first footman as she allowed herself to be handed out of the carriage.

She made her way up the marble steps to the porticoed entranceway. The door was immediately swung open by a most formidably dignified gentleman in elegant blue livery.

He stared down his nose for a moment at Anne and Tilly and then turned gracefully around without any word of greeting, leading them with great dispatch into the morning salon. He bowed himself out the door as he left them.

They looked at each other in consternation. After a nervous moment, Anne burst out laughing. "This is certainly an efficient establishment. The duchess must be a veritable tyrant."

Tilly nodded in a browbeaten agreement.

Anne shrugged and began to survey the room. It was very elegant indeed. It had quite a formal quality with its Louis XV *fauteuils*, its Louis XVI marble chimneypiece with a *biscuit de Sèvres* and ormolu clock on the mantel and its Aubusson rug.

Her exploration was interrupted by the entrance of a white-haired lady in a pink embroidered gown who came fluttering into the room.

The Duchess of Byrne was not at all what Anne expected. She was not built in Junoesque proportions; she was, instead, quite petite. She looked frail, as a matter of fact. Her face was curiously unlined, and her eyes were as blue as irises.

"Oh, here you are at last!" the duchess exclaimed, clapping her tiny hands together with unfeigned delight. "How remarkable. You don't look at all fagged. I was persuaded you'd be pulled to death by your long journey."

Anne blinked. "We stopped at an inn or two along the way, Your Grace."

"Oh, did you? How clever you are. I never stay at inns. I'm never able to find them when I need them. Let me take a look at you." She tilted her head as she took Anne's hands. "You are a pretty thing, aren't you? You must call me Aunt Honoria, you know. Actually, I'm your great-aunt-in-law, but that is a mouthful, isn't it? Only worse than 'Your Grace.' I should be used to that phrase by this time, but I always think it's referring to my husband. He's dead, you know. Been dead for many years. So you can well imagine how unsettling it is to think someone is addressing your late husband right to your very face."

Anne, wholly taken aback, was unable to think of a word to say. She could only nod in wide-eyed agreement.

"Yes, and if he took a look at you," this lady continued, "I'm sure he'd be unsettled, too. Fancied himself a lady's man, he did. Though I can't imagine why. He was balding, you know. And there's something terribly unromantic about balding gentlemen. Simon wasn't, was he?"

This direct question startled Anne, but she managed to shake her head in a negative reply.

"Well, of course not. It just goes to show you. Well, I hope you haven't brought many clothes with you," she said suddenly, eyeing with disfavor the clutched bandbox in Tilly's possession.

Anne was suddenly assailed by the horrible thought that the duchess was unwilling to have her stay. She embarked on a confused and stammering apology for imposing herself on the good lady, declaring that she had no intention of staying for long. She was ready to abandon her London plans then and there.

"Of course you are staying. But—" the duchess smiled sweetly "—I'm glad you haven't many clothes, because it shall be a great pleasure rigging you out in style. What a figure you have. It quite takes one's breath away. You can go upstairs and unpack." Anne jerked forward without thinking, and the duchess stopped her with a titter of laughter. "Not you, Anne. Your maid will be led to your room," she directed, carelessly dismissing Tilly, who, flustered, was promptly delivered into the hands of a footman. The duchess continued. "I'm persuaded you're parched and would be the better for a glass of ratafia. Then you may go upstairs and wash and change for dinner. Do you keep country hours? We eat at seven o'clock, but I told Cook to move tonight's meal up an hour or so. One must adjust oneself, you know."

Yes, indeed one must, Anne thought, finding it increasingly difficult to keep a straight face.

The duchess flitted to the bellpull and set it ringing, and the servant in the blue livery entered the room bowing.

"Bring us something restorative, Reeth," the duchess directed. "Something with spirits in it, if you know what I mean." The butler obviously did. He bowed out of the room without saying a word. "You aren't light-headed, are you?'' Lady Byrne asked, giving Anne an inquiring look.

"No," Anne said faintly, seriously doubting the veracity of her words.

The butler returned almost immediately, bearing a tray. He placed a glass within Anne's easy reach.

"And to think you're a widow," the duchess was saying. "No one would credit it. Some would say it's a pity you are one, but for myself, I'm heartily glad of it."

Anne, who had been taking a cautious sip of her ratafia, choked and looked up in surprise. "You are?" she exclaimed, in the liveliest astonishment. "Did you dislike Simon that much?"

The lady shook her head, putting a finger to her chin. "Why, no, I don't believe I disliked Simon at all. Never paid much attention to him. Did you?"

Anne was not forced to answer this disconcerting question, for the duchess continued. "I was far more interested in Max. He's such a delightful nephew." She sighed. "And it's a good thing I didn't pay much attention to Simon. Wouldn't I be in the suds if I did? Why, he's already dead!"

"How true. It was most wise on your part," Anne agreed.

"Well, would you call it wise? How unique. I've never been called that before. Many other things, mind you, but not wise." The duchess was excessively pleased with her compliment.

Rattle-pate, bagpipe, silly nodcock—a dozen other appellations rushed laughingly into Anne's mind, but she dismissed them all and decided the duchess was a darling.

"I'm glad you're a widow," the duchess persevered, "because I won't be forced to present you at the drawing rooms to the Queen or do any of the other tedious things sponsors for young debutantes are forced to do. We can concentrate on what's really important. Enjoying ourselves."

Anne had no doubt she would enjoy herself hugely and told the duchess as much. Lady Byrne squeezed her hand, blushed with pleasure, then shooed her away. "You must go up to your room. Mrs. Fardle will show you up."

Anne was led up to the blue bedchamber, a room that certainly lived up to its name. The wallpaper, carpet and even bed hangings were of a uniform, and monotonous, dark sapphire. Tilly was in the process of excavating from Anne's portmanteau her spare belongings, swimming in a veritable ocean of silver tissue wrapping as she placed the clothes tenderly into the wardrobe.

Anne thanked her for her efforts and declared, "I must hurry and change, or the cook will think I don't keep any hours, country or otherwise."

In less than twenty minutes Anne was dressed in a gown of stuffed muslin and ventured into the drawing room, seeking out her aunt. They then removed to the dining room, where Anne was regaled with a meal of several courses, the whole of which was spiced with the duchess's constant chatter.

"I do hope you found nothing amiss with your room, my dear. I have a decided partiality for that room myself. There's something oceanic about it."

"I wonder what it could be," Anne murmured. She had been thankful the walls themselves hadn't been painted blue as well, for just being in the room made her feel all at sea.

"Were you ever presented in London before, my dear? I can't recall, though that's no surprise."

"No," Anne replied. "I married Simon before I had really been released from the schoolroom. I had just turned eighteen."

"How clever of him to have found you, then. He was astute to have whisked you away before you'd had a Season, for no doubt you would have been swamped by suitors and beaux. Though that's not to say you won't be now. How diverting that will be. We'll probably have dozens of gentleman callers. And woman callers, too," she added conscientiously. "But, of course, they're not as interesting as men."

"I agree with you, Aunt Honoria," Anne said politely, though she couldn't help but think that the duchess herself, even though a female, was most interesting.

"Yes, but never having had a proper Season," the duchess continued as if she had never digressed, "you may find it uncomfortable being pitchforked into society. Especially since you don't know anyone. What I mean is, parties are most enjoyable, to be sure, but how much more enjoyable they are when you are assured of seeing at least one familiar face in the crowd. That's why I've decided to hold a rout for you. Nothing ostentatious, mind. Dancing, and some cards, of course, else none of the gentlemen will wish to come, and refreshments. The usual thing. About three hundred people or so."

"Three hundred!" Anne gasped, dropping her serviette.

The duchess tipped her head. "That is a paltry amount, I do admit. But what's the use of having a party to introduce you to some people if there are so many of them you can't remember their names?"

"What use at all?" Anne repeated, dazed.

"See? So I told you. We shall go over the guest list together if you wish, though I don't see what possible purpose that could serve, your not really knowing anyone in London."

Anne did know one person in London, and this person she was most desirous of meeting again at the first opportunity. "Well, I do know the Marquess of Crewe, Aunt Honoria," she said in a voice of studied indifference, her fork tracing patterns on her plate.

"How true. What a pleasure for you."

Anne would not have called it a pleasure, but she managed to smile agreeably and inquire, "He will be invited to the rout, will he not?"

"Why, of course he will," the lady asseverated in surprised accents. She gave Anne a reproachful look. "How could you think I would ever give a party without inviting dear Max? Yes," she sniffed, "*and* his most particular friends."

Now it was Anne's turn to be surprised. "Does he have friends?" she asked skeptically.

"Yes, I should think he does," the duchess declared, frowning at Anne's denseness. "There are too many to count, really, but his closest cronies are Lord Cecil Sherringham and Lord Ninian Wainfleet." She waved a tapering finger. "Oh, and he has recently taken a decided interest in young Geoffrey Stanhope, and I can well understand that, for Stanhope is the most diverting gentleman. Why, he never says a word, at least not to me he hasn't. He only bows and kisses my hand, and in the most nervous manner, you know.''

Anne wasn't surprised at hearing of a gentleman unable to say a word to the duchess. When would he get the chance? "You must be exaggerating, aunt.''

The duchess shook her head, considering this carefully, her brow knitted. "No, I don't believe I am. Though I did overhear a conversation he held with Max," she conceded. "It was all monosyllables, I assure you.''

Anne was impressed. "I can see how that type of conversationalist could be most fascinating.''

"Well, of course," the duchess agreed.

"What's Sherringham like?" Anne asked in a casual tone, but storing all this information most carefully away.

"Oh, excessively fat, truly. With the most liquid voice. And so lazy! He never puts himself out, not ever. I remember one evening he ensconced himself in a chair, and he never left it once. Quite changed the cushion's shape, really." She tapped her round chin with a finger. "Max says he has the liveliest mind in London. But I find that most difficult to believe. There's absolutely nothing lively about him that I can see.''

"Perhaps—" Anne gave a gurgle of laughter "—he finds the strain of his mental activities too much for him and must resort to physical inactivity to recoup his strength.''

"What an unusual idea," the duchess declared, diverted. "It might be true. I can't tell. You see, my mind never strains me at all.''

Anne took refuge in her Rhenish cream, mumbling an unsteady reply.

"But—" giving Sherringham his due "—he does have excellent sartorial taste. We shall ask his opinion on you when we've got you all rigged out." She was struck by a notion. "If Max were truly interested in lively minds, he would pay no attention to Lord Wainfleet. He really is a Ninian. I like him most excessively. He's very boyish. Quite delightful. I wonder how Max ever found him."

Anne doubted that any friend of Pastor Max's could be truly delightful. Unless, of course, the saying that opposites attract was true.

Seemingly engrossed with her dessert, Anne asked, "Does Lord Crewe have any special women friends?"

The duchess pondered this carefully. "It's hard to say, my dear. Most difficult. You see, he eschewed the fair sex ages ago."

Anne was startled. "He did what?"

"Wrote them off his list, if you know what I mean. It's understandable. He's had so many caps set at him in his career that he's soured on women. He was considered the best catch on the town," she said with simple pride. "He's so handsome, you know."

"And so rich," Anne said acidly. Otherwise she couldn't conceive why anyone would consider the bumptious Lord Crewe a catch.

"Yes," the duchess agreed affably. "Isn't it a pleasure being rich? But it was not a pleasure for Max to have so many women throwing themselves at him. So many nets and traps set up for him. It put him out of all patience."

"Well, why didn't he just marry and get it over with?" Anne had no sympathy for Crewe's plight.

"Daresay he never found anyone who suited him. He is rather fastidious."

Anne wrinkled her nose. "Niffynaffy, I'd say. A regular pattern-card of perfection." At least *he* thought so. But no brother of Simon's could be perfect.

"I'm sure he'd be pleased to hear you say so." The duchess smiled with innocent pleasure. "Max tries so hard to be a model of virtue."

This statement effectively deprived Anne of the remainder of her appetite.

After dinner, she followed the duchess into the salon, where Reeth had been instructed to gather together all the fashion periodicals in the house, a not inconsiderable pile, and place them on the secrétaire. Lady Byrne pounced upon them and promptly began to flip through the pages.

"We must set about planning your wardrobe," she explained, not turning her eyes from the fashion plates of *La Belle Assemblée*. "And your hair needs to be cut so Tidbury can fix it in the established modes. Have you any preferences in style?"

"I would like to try my hair à la Medusa," Anne said wistfully.

"Oh, no, I mean in walking dresses. Here's one with a green redingote. I don't think that would become you at all." Anne had a fleeting glimpse of a wisp of a model in a green confection. "I think green with yellow hair—or gold, rather—would be quite bilious. Though I do think this parasol is pretty."

The duchess, in her confusing but enthusiastic way, initiated Anne into the intricacies of London fashion. Anne became quite eager for the morrow, which, as the duchess assured her, would be a delightful adventure for the two of them, for they were going to brave Bond Street.

The duchess caught Anne covering a surreptitious yawn and clapped her hands. "There. I knew you must have been exhausted by your long journey. You must go to sleep at once. You'll need your energy for tomorrow."

Anne complied with her directions readily enough, giving the dear lady a kiss on the cheek and wishing her an affectionate good-night.

She dismissed the maid and Tilly from her room and changed into her nightwear unassisted. She wished to have some privacy in which to digest the exciting events that had occurred to her.

She didn't know about Pastor Max, but her own life had certainly taken a turn for the better and had become most lively. She hoped she was up to all the excitement. Why, a London Season was an endless round of balls, routs, drums, assemblies and even Venetian breakfasts. Not at all what she was used to. To be sure, her life with Simon had not been particularly dull, but neither had it been pleasant. Her face became serious. Her elopement had been the worst mistake of her life. She had been a foolish little schoolgirl with dreams of adventure and romance. Anne sighed. But she was not one to repine. Everything she had endured with Simon, from sneaking out of hotels in the dead of night to avoid paying their shot to having to endure the hot and amorous advances of Simon's card partners, had seemed, even at the time, to be happening to someone else, not herself at all. As though she were living a dream. *A nightmare, more like,* she thought with a grimace. But that was all over. For here she was, afloat in the blue bedchamber with nothing more daunting to expect on the morrow than a trip down Bond Street and nothing more dangerous to consider than her planned assault on Pastor Max. She grinned mischievously. If the poor fellow knew what was planned for him, he would take to his heels.

But the next day, Anne realized that if she had known what the Duchess of Byrne had planned for her, she herself would have taken to her heels. Not that it was so terrible. Just exhausting.

The two, with Tom Groom on the box, set off in the carriage for Bond Street, ready to ransack the town— or so, at least, the duchess intended. They went from factory to factory, rummaging through silks, satins and brocades. Lengths and lengths of material were held up to Anne to see if they were becoming to her complexion. Lady Byrne felt that Anne looked beautiful in all shades, a sentiment breathlessly concurred in by the smitten clerks who waited on them. Since Anne was a widow, she was not limited to whites and insipid pastels. Oh, no. She was able to indulge, and indulge she would, in the richest golds, the deepest blues and the warmest emeralds. Anne paused thoughtfully over a scarlet taffeta.

"It would look most dashing as a riding coat," Lady Byrne suggested.

"I was considering having it made up as an evening gown."

Lady Byrne stared at her in frozen silence for a full minute—probably the longest moment of silence in her life. "Anne," she said finally and in awful accents, "a scarlet evening gown would be most improper. Why—" and she gasped at her own audacity "—it would make you look just like a high-flyer."

One of the dressier types of prostitute on the town. Anne's face hardened and her hand tightened into a fist as she recalled that Pastor Max had called her just that, a high-flyer.

"Well, Aunt Honoria, don't you think it would start a new fashion?"

"But," Lady Byrne protested, "there's nothing new about high-flyers, my dear. I believe they've been around forever. And I really don't think we should be going on in this way." She looked nervously about. "Especially not in public," she whispered.

Anne laughed and let the subject drop, determined to have a private conference with Madame Franchot, the high-class modiste in Bruton Street patronized by Lady Byrne.

Before visiting the dressmaker, however, they ventured into the Soho Bazaar, a veritable Aladdin's cave of riches and furbelows. Anne was induced to purchase silk stockings, reticules and gloves. Lady Byrne, beside herself with pleasure, pressed upon Anne branches of artificial flowers, ells of ribbons and piles of spangled silk scarves and embroidered shawls. Tom Groom soon found himself struggling under a mountain of bandboxes and packages.

Madame Franchot greeted the Duchess of Byrne and her protégée, the Lady Severne, with all due deference. But respect for the duchess's rank was not what inspired the dressmaker to fall into rhapsodies over Lady Severne's lovely figure. She knew just how to set it off to advantage, and she sent her assistant, Miss Mudford, for her sketches of all her à la mode fashions. Why, this ball gown with the Russian bodice would be just the thing. And the three-quarter dress of diamanté silk fastened down the center with diamonds would be ravishing. And surely she would be irresistible in a morning dress with Circassian sleeves and in an opera gown with ruched flounces.

Anne approved of all of Madame Franchot's designs and even suggested an improvement where the décolletage of the gowns was concerned.

"Make them as low as feasible, *madame*," she stated with decision.

Madame Franchot gave a roguish grin. "Oh, *la coquette*. She will turn all the men's heads."

"But of course she will," the duchess defended her charge. "With or without a low décolletage." She wavered. "But perhaps not too low."

Madame and Anne exchanged knowing glances. And Madame was in perfect agreement over the possibilities of a red evening gown. "The style must be simple. As simple as possible. Yet it shall be most daring."

"Too daring by half," Lady Byrne grumbled, but was too busy planning their next stop at the milliner's to put up more than a halfhearted protest.

At the end of the day, Anne tottered into the duchess's house in Grosvenor Square certain she would be unable to muster enthusiasm over anything ever again. Unless, of course, it was for a long and uninterrupted night's sleep.

This was granted her, but the very next morning her hot chocolate was followed by a visit from Alexander, a rather silly, frippery fellow with mincing ways who turned out to be a magician with hair.

Anne's tresses were ruthlessly cropped. Yes, her hair was of a most poetical blond color, just like guineas, in fact, and yes, it was as soft as spun flax, but it had no theme, no theme at all. It must be cut. And cut it was. Tidbury was called upon to display her talents in styling hair under Alexander's critical gaze. She was on her mettle and whipped Anne's hair into several breathtaking versions of the Sappho and even won Alexander's approbation with her Medusa.

Boxes and boxes of finished dresses began to be delivered to the house, much to Lady Byrne's delight, and as the night of the rout party approached, her spirits rose and rose, almost to fever pitch. The Duchess of Byrne, completely unlike her odious nephew, seemed to gain the greatest enjoyment out of life.

"And as for jewelry," she declared as the thought occurred to her, "I, of course, make you free of my vaults. I've got some pretty pieces, though my diamond tiara is too heavy and gives me a headache, and my emerald necklace is quite Gothic. But I do think you'll like my sapphires. As a matter of fact, I think they match your eyes. It's a pity your eyes aren't red. I mean, because my set of rubies are so acclaimed, you know."

Anne tried to refuse this kind offer, feeling overwhelmed. "I would be quite terrified to wear diamonds, Aunt Honoria."

"No, would you? How unusual." She took Anne's hand and gave it a tight squeeze. "But I trust you implicitly, dear, so you needn't consider your scruples."

"I must," she stammered.

"But you're here for a Season in London. And you can't have any scruples," the lady declared with worldly wisdom. She winked at Anne. "Especially if you wish to trap for yourself some gentleman."

Anne certainly did wish to trap for herself some gentleman, so, with a secret smile, she acquiesced in Lady Byrne's wishes.

CHAPTER THREE

ON THE EVENING of the rout party, Anne stepped into the drawing room to wait for Lady Byrne. She had taken great pains with her toilette and was entrancingly attired in a robe of jonquil crepe with velvet ribbons spangled with gold. The duchess's diamond necklace was clasped about her throat, and a diamond crescent was set in her golden hair. Lord Crewe, nothing if not a proper nephew, had sent bouquets of flowers to both Anne and Lady Byrne. Anne had provocatively placed one of the white roses from her bouquet at the bosom of her gown, hoping Max would appreciate its place of honor.

She came out just as Lady Byrne wandered down the stairs. The duchess was wearing an evening gown of white-and-silver gauze. A train of purple velvet was gathered behind her, enveloping the staircase. Upon her sweet head reposed a tiara of diamonds—the heavy one that gave her a headache. She looked magnificent.

"Oh, Aunt Honoria," Anne cried, running up to her and giving her an impulsive hug, "you look wonderful."

Lady Byrne was pleased. "You think so, dear?" she asked. "I am so happy to hear it. Only this train is such a bother. I keep hoping to lose it, but no, it still stays behind me."

"And it had best stay behind you, dear aunt," Anne said in a serious tone belied only by the twinkle in her eye. "It makes you look an imposing figure."

Lady Byrne was impressed by this accolade and preened herself a little as she awaited the arrival of her guests.

Anne wondered what the night would hold in store for her. Having been forced to sit through a daunting conning of Lady Byrne's guest list, she knew she would be mingling with quite a number of the beau monde tonight. She certainly hoped she wouldn't rub them the wrong way. But her first concern was not with the sort of impression she would make at this her first party. No, not at all. She was determined to make this a debut of a different sort—the debut of Max's career as a libertine. She chuckled as she thought of the shocked expression on his face if ever he heard himself called a libertine. It would be a study of outraged virtue. But what was sauce for the goose was sauce for the gander, she thought militantly. She hadn't liked being called a trollop! She wondered how his new career would suit him. She had no doubt it wouldn't suit him at all, but it would suit her perfectly.

She then pondered on just how to introduce Pastor Max to his new career, but her lucubrations were interrupted by the arrival of the first guests. The ballroom doors were swung open by two footmen to receive them.

The mirrors of the ballroom wall had been polished and the hundreds of candles in the sparkling chandeliers reflected scintillatingly against them. In the adjoining dining room, tables were laden with cakes and champagne. All was set for an evening of dancing and pleasure. The rooms began to fill to overflowing, and the rout party commenced.

Anne was delighted by the color and vivacity of the people she met, but one gentleman won her unqualified disapprobation.

"Who is that odd-looking gentleman in the pink coat?" Anne inquired of Lady Byrne of a rail-thin fellow wearing a silk coat and high heels. As he approached them, Anne was able to observe the debauchery of his countenance, which was heavily lined and had sunken red eyes under penciled eyebrows. His thin lips curled distastefully.

"That is Lord Cyprian Denzil," Lady Byrne whispered back. "He's a notable rake but is acceptable to society because of his vast fortune."

He was certainly not acceptable to Anne. As she held out her hand in greeting, her smile froze in revulsion. Denzil not only bent and kissed her hand with a lingering, wet kiss, but he also tickled her palm with his finger. She eyed him with hostility and was only prevented from giving him a ringing set-down by the number of other guests pressing upon her for her attention.

Anne had the felicity of being greeted kindly by everyone. A Lord Epworth, a Mr. Dunston and a Lord Denmore were all very profuse in their compliments, eagerly pressing her hand and striving to claim it for a dance.

But Anne was assured of being a success when the thin and willowy Lady Jersey, one of the patronesses of Almack's, exclaimed in pleasure at the sight of Lady Byrne's protégée. In the first words she uttered she promised to give Anne a voucher to Almack's.

"I daresay you won't be much interested in attending Almack's." She smiled. "Not being a debutante and all that nonsense. But I can assure you there will be a number of gentlemen who will be most interested in having you attend Almack's. To make your acquaintance and all that."

Anne thanked her prettily, and Lady Jersey departed into the ballroom. Lady Byrne clasped Anne's hand. "You will like Almack's, I've no doubt of it," she bubbled with obvious gratification. "It's got a sort of *je ne sais quoi* about it. You'll see."

Anne nodded, trying to appear duly enthusiastic despite her indifference to Almack's and to Lady Jersey. The marriage mart held little interest for her. She had other fish to fry during her Season. And—her eyes widened now with tingling anticipation—here, if she was not mistaken, was the gullible fish she was angling for.

The Marquess of Crewe, little aware that he was being viewed as a fish, was slowly making his way up the steps, holding his hand out to the Duchess of Byrne. He moved languidly and gracefully. He was dressed to perfection in a very natty coat of black superfine that seemed molded to his massive shoulders. In the snowy folds of his Mathematical neckcloth reposed a chaste pearl.

"You look complete to a shade, my lord," Anne murmured provocatively.

He turned to her slowly and put up his quizzing glass, superciliously studying her through it. Knowing she looked her best, Anne put up a defiant chin, refusing to be daunted by his critical scrutiny.

"I daresay," he murmured finally. "It's a way I have. You, of course, look very well."

Anne snorted at this tepid compliment. "Lord Epworth thinks I look ravishing," she huffed.

Lady Byrne, attending their conversation, struck in. "Very true, Max. He said so. And he's not one to pay attention to anyone's looks but his own."

Crewe was unimpressed. "Considering he is known as one of the Dandy set and succumbs to all their worst affectations, from outrageously high shirt points to the draping of his person with fobs and trinkets, a compliment from him is not worth crowing about, my dear Lady Anne. His taste is so lamentable."

Anne fumed. "I was also complimented by Lord Denmore and Mr. Dunston," she informed him defiantly.

"So you've won their hearts, too, have you?" He lifted his eyebrow distastefully. "Fast work, my dear lady. I hope you don't intend to set the ton on its ears with any other type of fast behavior at this ball."

Her eyes narrowed. "Of what type?" she asked in a dangerously quiet voice.

"Oh, you know, Anne," chimed in Lady Byrne. "Things like standing up with the same gentleman more than twice for a dance. Or, heaven forbid, walking out on the terrace alone with a gentleman. Or, or..." She cast about, somewhat at a loss. She turned to the marquess for assistance.

"Or," he said dampeningly, "letting yourself be condemned as a flirt."

Anne shrugged indifferently. "I don't find Lord Epworth or Lord Denmore or Mr. Dunston interesting enough to flirt with."

"Such sentiments do you honor, my lady," Max sneered. "No doubt if they did interest you, such considerations as propriety and decorum would be flung aside without a thought.''

''But of course,'' Anne agreed sweetly.

Crewe's mouth snapped shut, and he swung on his heels back to Lady Byrne. He kissed her hand and thanked her for honoring him by carrying the bouquet he had sent her. He then cast a disdainful eye at the white rose placed so demurely at Anne's breast and pointedly made no comment. With a bow, he departed.

Anne greeted the next few guests absently, wanting to escape the receiving line to follow Max. After a short time, she whispered in Lady Byrne's ear, ''Do you think, Aunt Honoria, that I could be excused from the receiving line?''

''Oh, but of course you may,'' the duchess cried. ''How stupid of me not to realize you'd be eager for some dancing. And, no doubt, that there'll be gentlemen here eager to dance with you. But I'm not surprised I didn't think of it, because I dance so little myself. It's such a bother, my dear. I always get dizzy doing the waltz. And in the country-dances and cotillions, I always forget my steps. And that, you must know, is mortifying in the extreme.''

Anne nodded and rushed away before Lady Byrne could animadvert at length on all the dances she had mulled in her long career.

She made straight for the ballroom.

The Pandean Pipes were already playing, and couples were whirling about the dance floor. When Anne stepped into the room, she was instantly besieged by Beaux and Pinks of the ton, all of whom were desirous of soliciting her hand for the dance.

Anne hesitated, eyeing through their clustered and pomaded heads the prospects before her. Those who were not dancing were chatting with acquaintances or eyeing the other occupants of the room. A number of dowagers were sitting in chairs lined up against the wall, and most of them were now watching Anne with expressions of severe disapproval on their faces. Since she was a widow, no doubt they expected Anne to take her place among them. But Anne didn't feel like a widow, and she certainly had no intention of behaving like one.

With a defiant spark in her eyes, she put her hand on the arm nearest her and smiled up into the face of the lucky gentleman. It was Lord Denmore, who was smiling at her, his round face flushed with triumph. He snapped his fingers at the disappointed gentlemen nearby and led Anne onto the floor.

The waltz had finished and the musicians were just striking up a country-dance, so Anne was not forced to hold more than a cursory conversation with her partner as she was swept up into the set. She allowed her eyes to wander, searching for Pastor Max. It was not long before she sighted her prey. He was leaning negligently against a pillar, holding a desultory conversation with some young buck. She turned her head quickly before he could catch her staring. She had no wish to let him think she was taking an undue interest in him. She forced herself, for the time being, to ignore his presence and, meeting Lord Denmore's gaze once more, smiled up at him most enchantingly, no doubt causing his heart to race with pleasure.

When the set was finished, Denmore led her to a chair so that she could rest herself from the exertions of the dance and offered to bring her a glass of iced champagne.

"How very kind of you," she murmured, unfurling her fan and fluttering it before her face, her eyes peeping above it at Denmore most coquettishly. "I would be vastly obliged to you."

He caught his breath and stared at her a moment as though bewitched; then he gave a start and hurried away to the refreshment tables.

"What a display," snorted a disgusted voice.

Anne did not turn her head. "I'm glad you took such interest in it, Lord Crewe."

"Don't flatter yourself," he said shortly. "I'm only concerned with how your actions will reflect on me."

Her fan stopped its motions, for she was a little unnerved. Did he suspect that she intended to commit a number of actions that would, most unpleasantly, reflect on him? "Why should anything I take it into my head to do reflect on you?" she asked in an indifferent tone. She looked up and found he was leaning down toward her, his face quite close to her own. She jerked back, feeling the blood rush to her cheeks.

"You are my sister-in-law, remember?" he reminded her sardonically, his eyes glinting. "You mentioned that distasteful fact not so long ago."

"True. But though we're related, there's absolutely no family resemblance between us," she said facetiously, and his eyebrows lowered in a frown.

"Thank God for that."

"I've no doubt you do," she sniffed pettishly. "Oh, do go away." She waved her fan at him. "You needn't hover over me like a watchdog. Do you think I'm going to commit some indiscretion sitting here?"

"Considering your unprincipled character," he said coldly, "I wouldn't be surprised if you did."

Her eyes snapped. Oh, he wouldn't, would he? She stood up resolutely and approached Mr. Dunston, a dark-haired lad who was hanging about hopefully. His brown eyes lighted up at her approach, and he nearly fell over himself as he begged, in a stammering voice, her hand for the dance. "I would be most honored, you know," he gushed.

She smiled her acquiescence and stepped onto the floor, completely ignoring the marquess who was glowering after her.

Wouldn't be surprised if she committed some indiscretion, hmm? Well, she wouldn't dream of disappointing him. She gave her partner an appraising look, and her eyes began to twinkle wickedly.

"Mr. Dunston," she said suddenly, startling this gentleman into a misstep, "don't you find it rather stifling on the dance floor?"

"I suppose . . . I hadn't thought . . ." he stammered. He gulped and took a breath. "Do you?" he asked anxiously.

"Dreadfully so," she declared.

He nodded, with a sinking face. "Shall I lead you off the floor?" he asked dismally.

"Please do," she agreed promptly. "But not back to my chair, if you please. I am so overcome by the heat that I feel I can be restored to comfort only if I am blessed with a breath of fresh air."

Mr. Dunston, somewhat at a loss, stammered, "Yes, I can well understand your feelings—"

"So if you would be so kind, lead me out onto the terrace."

He came to a dead halt at these words and gulped convulsively, gaping at her in astonishment before he collected himself. Then his eyes gleamed, and his face became wreathed in smiles at this most unexpected treat. "Of course I shall," he declared with alacrity.

He then hastened her off the dance floor, heading for the terrace. Anne swung her gaze around and caught the eye of the Marquess of Crewe, who, sure enough, was watching her with a glowering expression. She gave him a pert smile and sauntered onto the terrace, her hand on Dunston's arm.

There were Chinese lamps hung about most festively, their light rivaling that of the moon. Anne stopped, screening herself behind a curtain. Mr. Dunston, who had set his sights on a marble bench placed within a very private arbor of trees, was surprised and looked down at her with a questioning expression on his face.

"I think, Mr. Dunston," Anne said demurely, "that my recovery would be much hastened if you were to bring me a glass of iced champagne."

He assimilated her words slowly. His shoulders drooped in resignation as he gave a polite nod. "Your servant," he murmured in a stifled voice. He started back to the doorway through which they had entered, but Anne stopped him. She pointed to an archway a few feet up.

"I think you'll reach the refreshment tables more easily through that entrance," she suggested kindly. He nodded and hurried forward, disappearing through the doorway just as the Marquess of Crewe burst upon her looking mad as fire.

She started to move away but was swung forcibly around by the enraged marquess.

"I thought you were told it was most improper to stroll on the terrace alone with a gentleman," he almost shouted, glaring down at her. His face was red and his mouth twisted.

She shrugged out of his grasp. "So I was," she acknowledged with the greatest unconcern.

He seethed at her flippant air and swung his gaze threateningly about. "Where is Mr. Dunston?" he demanded.

"Why, he's getting me a glass of champagne."

The change in his expression was ludicrous. His eyes goggled. "You mean *we* are here alone?"

She bit her lip to keep from laughing. Schooling her countenance with difficulty, she stared at him, allowing growing suspicion to widen her eyes. In a shaking voice, she said, "Oh, pretty subtle of you, Lord Crewe, to trick me out here all alone with you." She shook her finger at him accusingly. "For some indiscretion, no doubt. Are you meaning to wheedle a kiss out of me?"

He was so taken aback that he nearly reeled. "I! You must be all about in your head. I would never do such a thing."

She clearly did not believe him. She shook her head at him reproachfully, then pretended to consider carefully the situation she was in. She put her hand to her chin. "If I allowed you to kiss me, it would be a very fast thing to do, would it not? But since we are alone and no one can see us, as we are screened by a curtain, who could say it was fast? The curtain?"

He glared at her, a heightened color staining his cheeks. "*I* would say it was fast," he nearly exploded.

"But you would never be so ungentlemanly as to disclose to the world a poor widow's mild indiscretions, would you?" she exclaimed, giving him a glance of burning reproach.

"A poor widow?" he scoffed, flinging up his arms. "You're wicked. Most wicked."

"It's better than being ungentlemanly," she said hotly. "So you'd better hurry and take the kiss you've been so clever as to trick from me and then go about your business." She sniffed and said in a most aggrieved tone, "I do think you're a very odd sort of brother-in-law. You warn me against social solecisms at the same time that you're demanding one from me."

"I'm not demanding anything from you!" he burst out, nearly shaking with anger. "Except that you return to the dance floor at once."

"Ah." She nodded with sudden comprehension. "Forgive me for so wronging you, my lord. You'd like to waltz with me, that's what it is." She smiled with relief. "I daresay I can reconcile my conscience with that innocuous act." She shook her head at him again. "You really needn't have gone to such lengths to procure my hand for the dance, you know. I'm not that averse to dancing with you. You needn't have stooped to blackmail, my lord."

He looked thunderstruck. "What?"

"Tricking me to stand for a length of time alone with you on the terrace was most reprehensible," she chided. "But I'll engage to dance the waltz with you if you promise not to tell anyone of my lapse."

"But, I don't want to waltz with you!" he declared with all the appearance of a man being goaded beyond his endurance.

"So it must be a kiss?" She looked dismayed. Then she shrugged philosophically. "Oh, well, I'm willing to sacrifice myself."

"Oh, are you?" he snapped. Then he took a deep breath and regained his composure with a visible effort. "I, on the other hand, am not willing to sacrifice myself." And he swung around to make good his escape only to collide full tilt with Lady Jersey, who was strolling arm in arm with her friend the social lioness Mrs. Drummond-Burrell. Both ladies eyed him with a good deal of astonishment not unmixed with condemnation. Max flushed to the roots of his hair.

Anne, feeling that her cup was running over, sauntered forward as if to leave the terrace, only to stop dead in her tracks in flustered embarrassment at being confronted with these two ladies.

She tittered nervously and gasped, "Oh, dear," making her eyes as round as saucers and putting her hand to her mouth.

Max ran a finger under his collar, looking considerably harassed.

Mrs. Drummond-Burrell looked Anne up and down, an expression of distaste lengthening her already long features. Anne managed to look quite guilty under her scathing scrutiny, casting her eyes to the ground and biting her lip.

Lady Jersey, tugging at her friend's round arm, clucked audibly and shook her finger admonishingly at Max. Then both ladies put up their chins and marched away, censure plain in their stiffened backs.

Max stared at Anne for one burning moment. "Well!" he burst out. "I hope you're satisfied." Then he stalked away to take shelter in the card room on the ground floor.

Anne was indeed satisfied. It was all she could do to suppress an unbecoming smirk. Her plot was working. Feeling heady with success, she followed Max into the gaming room, intent upon continuing with her own game.

She paused at the door to survey the players. It gave her a frisson of excitement to note that she was the only female in the room.

She caught sight of Max seating himself at a table in the corner of the room, with the oddest set of cronies it had ever been her fortune to see. As though drawn by a magnet, she made straight for the table, eyeing Max's companions with undisguised fascination. These must be the gentlemen Lady Byrne had described to her.

A dark-haired man of massive girth was almost lying on a frail Pendleton chair, his great weight causing this innocent seat to appear a most precarious and dangerous perch indeed. It looked as though it might collapse underneath him at any moment. The large gentleman, however, appeared unconscious of the danger he was in. In fact, he seemed almost physically unconscious. His face, with its aquiline nose and rounded cheeks, tilted forward, and his eyelids drooped heavily. He looked, for all the world, fast asleep. Anne only realized that he was not asleep when he spoke suddenly in a liquid, almost gurgling, voice.

"Stanhope," murmured Lord Sherringham wearily, "turn over that card for me, if you would be so very kind."

Young Stanhope, a tall, thin fellow with mouse-brown hair, was so very kind, and he promptly turned over the indicated card. The card was a club. Lord Ninian Wainfleet, Sherringham's opponent, slapped down a quarte with an expectant look on his animated face.

"Stanhope—" Sherringham sighed "—could you hand me my glass of canary? I need a diversion while I ponder what next move to make."

The glass was placed within his plump grasp, and he bowed his head to take meditative sips. Anne waited, alive with curiosity to see if he would actually make another move. She was not disappointed when he signed Stanhope to hand him a card from the pile lying on the table and Stanhope bent to oblige him. What an odd way of moving.

Lord Ninian Wainfleet appeared to be accustomed to Sherringham's unusual method of conducting a card game and waited, without the least sign of impatience, until the next card was placed, by Stanhope, upon the table.

"A king, is it?" he cried, his pale blue eyes sparkling. His hand scratched his very blond locks, contributing to their already disordered state. "I'll show you." And with that, he slapped down a diamond.

Anne took hold of her courage, fetched a deep breath and stepped forward. Max watched her approach with evident alarm. Before he could say a word or before Sherringham could wave a lazy finger to Stanhope, she said in a penetrating voice, "Do you mind if I join your game?"

Her words fell upon the gentlemen like a bombshell. Ninian uttered a shocked gasp, starting from his chair. Stanhope, staring like a gapeseed, began stuttering incoherently. Sherringham was so powerfully affected that he ventured to snap his glass on the table without any assistance. Only Lord Crewe appeared unmoved. He just sat, staring grimly at this fair intruder.

Ninian recovered first. He asked, his face still alive with incredulity, "Did you say you wished to join us in a game of cards? I don't think we could possibly have heard you aright."

Anne, who had endured many interminable evenings trapped at a card table with her husband and who had vowed never to go near a gaming table ever again in her entire life, said, "Yes."

"Yes, what?"

"Yes, you heard me correctly," she said with a coolness she was far from feeling. "And yes, I would care to join you in a game of chance. How perfectly kind of you to invite me."

"But I don't think we did, did we?" Ninian demanded of Mr. Stanhope. That very correct, very polite gentleman, who would never dream of offending a lady, gave Ninian a reproachful look.

Ninian mopped his brow, looking all on end. He took a deep breath. "But this is not silver-loo, ma'am. It's piquet."

"What a relief." Anne smiled, her eyes twinkling. "I can't abide loo. A more insipid game I've never been forced to endure."

Ninian was so much in agreement with these sentiments that he could not think of a single word to say.

Finding the gentlemen still tending to gape at her, she smiled at them mockingly. "What, shall I set off a challenge to anyone?" She looked directly at Lord Crewe.

Ninian, an impetuous fellow, intervened. "Oh, Crewe wouldn't think of engaging in a game of chance with a lady. He's a high stickler."

"How true." She nodded. "You are a high stickler, aren't you, Pastor Max?"

Geoffrey Stanhope gasped. And Ninian, biting his lip, asked in an unsteady voice, "Wh-what did you call him?"

Max could suppress his anger no longer. "Of all the brass-faced little gypsies!" he exploded. "How dare you ask to play cards with us?" He pointed furiously at the doorway. "Leave this room at once, I insist!"

Anne cocked a knowing eye and looked at Ninian. "See. He *is* a Pastor Max."

Ninian was silent for one breathless moment, and then he nearly exploded with laughter. "It's so apt," he sputtered.

Max cast him a quelling look. "I'm nothing of the kind. But—" he frowned darkly "—I do know what is considered proper and what is not. It would be most improper for you to engage in a game of chance with three strange gentlemen."

Not even Sherringham liked hearing himself described as "strange," and he ventured to murmur a mild protest. "I say, Max. Would you call me strange?"

Max bit his lip. He saw that Stanhope, too, was casting him a deprecating glance, and he choked down a sudden laugh. "Oh, don't fly up into the boughs, gentlemen. I had no intention of offending you."

Sherringham, much mollified, gave an imperceptible nod, and Max turned his attention back to Anne.

She was unrepentant. "Since you are my brother-in-law, perhaps you can act as my chaperon. I'm sure it's a role that would suit you to perfection."

Max, his face filled with outrage, almost burst out with a disclaimer but was interrupted by a tug on his arm. It was Ninian, who directed a curious look at Anne. "She's your sister-in-law? Perhaps you would introduce us."

Stanhope stood up to do honor to the occasion, and Sherringham went so far as to sit up straight in his chair.

Max cast a fulminating look at Anne, but he performed the requested introduction. "May I make known to you, Lady Severne, Mr. Stanhope, Lord Sherringham and Lord Wainfleet. Gentlemen, this is Simon's widow. The Lady Anne Severne."

Ninian held out a ready hand, shaking hers most vigorously. Stanhope, much too shy to shake hands with any lady, coughed, cleared his throat and bowed.

Sherringham tipped his head a trifle. "Charmed."

"Now that you've so thoroughly interrupted the game, perhaps you would be so good as to leave this company at once."

Anne was unimpressed by his imperious tone. She cast an imploring look at Stanhope and Ninian. "But then I would be left with nothing to do but dance. Most insipid stuff, don't you agree?"

Ninian, much struck, said, "Yes, I can quite see her point. It would be too bad to waste an entire evening waltzing about in circles. And having to hold a conversation with some nodcock of a partner at the same time."

Mr. Stanhope, who had endured many agonizing moments on a dance floor trying to achieve that impossible feat, nodded feelingly.

"Why don't you let her join us, Max?" Sherringham requested after a short pause. He considered it much too strenuous to engage in an argument of any sort, let alone listen to one, and he tried to speak soothingly. "Stanhope, please be so good as to pull out a chair for Lady Anne."

Stanhope readily did so, and with a triumphant flush, Anne took her seat at the table. She smiled gratefully at Sherringham and asked politely, "Will it tire you too greatly, Lord Sherringham, to engage in a three-handed game?"

He considered this carefully. He sighed. "If Stanhope is up to it, then so am I." Stanhope nodded his willingness, and Max flung himself back in his chair, much disgruntled. He muttered to himself. Not much reached Anne's ears, but such overheard scraps as "vixen . . . gypsy . . . wicked" were enough to bring an angry spark to her eyes.

Ninian looked to be most diverted by the turn of events. He was obviously ready to approve of any relative of Max's, and he smiled engagingly at Anne as he dealt the cards. She noticed that Max refrained from taking up a hand.

"Is there no way we can induce Pastor Max to join us?" she inquired of no one in particular. "I'm sure there's something he'd like to win from me. Perhaps I should issue a personal challenge to him. Play or pay. If I win in a hand of piquet, my lord, you'd be obliged to introduce me to all the most eligible *partis* in the ton—just throw me in their way, so to speak."

His face became grim. "No matter how much it would please me to have you off my hands, I wouldn't think of being so inhuman. It would be cruel and unfair to lead any man into your toils, madam."

"Are you hanging out for a husband?" Ninian demanded suddenly.

"Isn't everyone?"

"I'm not, dash it," he exclaimed, looking revolted.

Mr. Stanhope clucked and turned red.

"I should hope not," murmured Sherringham. "Otherwise I'd be forced to recommend that you be placed under restraint."

Ninian, becoming aware of the import of his words, flushed with discomfiture. "You know what I mean," he said hastily.

"Of course we do," Anne soothed him.

"Well, but what a dashed dull way of spending the Season. There are too many other things to do to waste your time trying to make a connection."

"Such as?"

Ninian shrugged, casting about. "Spar with Jackson at his Sparring Saloon. Bet on the horses at Tattersall's. Blow a cloud at Cribb's Parlor. Drink blue ruin—"

"Vauxhall's," burst out Mr. Stanhope.

"And don't forget Watier's," breathed Lord Sherringham. He rolled his eyes. "They give the best dinners in town."

"Yes," Ninian agreed.

Anne opened her eyes innocently wide. "Does Max do any of these things?" she inquired, unable to resist smiling a little slyly at Lord Crewe.

They considered this carefully. "Why, no," Ninian said finally. "He doesn't." His eyes brightened at a sudden thought. "He does go to Watier's every so often." Doubt shook him. "But that's only to keep Sherringham company, I daresay."

Anne shook her head pityingly. "What a dull dog."

"Well, not dull precisely," Ninian temporized. "Just fastidious."

"That's what I meant." Anne smiled.

Max looked as though it would have given him the greatest pleasure to box her ears. Through gritted teeth, he said, "Might I suggest you leave off talking of me and turn to the game you were so anxious to engage in?"

"Oh, yes." She turned brightly to Ninian. "What are the stakes?"

"Oh, we're playing for love."

She pooh-poohed this. "That's much too pedestrian," she protested. "We must wager something," she declared. "Just to enliven the game, you know."

Ninian and Sherringham expressed themselves ready to acquiesce in her wishes.

"Now, what can I put up for stakes?" Anne wondered. "Let me see." She put her hand tentatively to her bosom, casting a sidelong glance at Max from beneath her lashes. She caressed herself absently. Max looked sick with apprehension. "My—"

He started up from his chair. "Have you no sense of propriety?" he shouted, quite red in the face.

She blinked at him. "But I was only going to put up my flower." She indicated the white rose he had given her, pinned at her breast.

He seethed, angry at himself for being taken in. "You're wicked!" he ejaculated.

"Is she, by gad?" Ninian looked interested. "But all she did was wager her rose, you know."

"*And* try to trick me into giving her a kiss behind a curtain!" Max declared, exposing her iniquity to the world.

"Well, I say!" Ninian exclaimed. All three gentlemen put up their quizzing glasses and eyed Anne with undisguised admiration. "You *are* a wicked widow, ain't you?"

CHAPTER FOUR

ANNE AWOKE to discover that her debut into the world of the ton had been an unqualified success. All morning long, the house was deluged by visitors, bouquets, cards and posies—all for her.

Around noon she walked into the salon in time to give her greetings to Lady Jersey, who was just bringing her morning visit to a close. Both Lady Byrne and Lady Jersey appeared a trifle red in the face, as though the exertion of holding a tête-à-tête, with each trying to dominate the conversation, had been quite exhausting.

Lady Jersey, who possessed the misleading sobriquet of "Silence," rose dramatically from her chair at the sight of Anne, holding out her hands in greeting. She was dressed to perfection in a rose-pink muslin gown. "Oh, dear Lady Anne," she exclaimed hastily before Lady Byrne could say a word, "I've just been telling the duchess what a phenomenal success you are. I've had numberless gentlemen begging me for an introduction to you; it is quite diverting. But I knew just how it would be, as I told you last night." She smiled smugly. "I don't think any lady has made such a hit since Miss Gunning arrived in town. You remember Miss Gunning, don't you, Honoria?" she asked, and continued talking without waiting for a reply, although Lady Byrne had taken a deep breath, prepar-

tled herself on the sofa with the flowers held to her nose. Ah, what a delightful scent.

Lady Jersey noticed this action and gave a quizzing smile. "I see you favor Lord Epworth's suit above all others," she observed with a significant lift to her eyebrows.

Anne looked puzzled. Then she held up the flowers, comprehension sinking in. "Oh, because of the flowers. Oh, dear, what an intrigant you are, Lady Jersey," she chided. "I don't admire Lord Epworth. I just admire his choice of flowers."

"Yes, they go prettily with your yellow gown," approved Lady Byrne. She turned to Lady Jersey, militant pride in her face. "Anne has such unerring good taste, you see. I don't think she could ever develop a *tendre* for such a caper merchant as Lord Epworth," she declared, wrinkling her tiny nose.

"Have you developed a *tendre* for anyone at all, Lady Anne?" inquired Lady Jersey with a roguish glint in her eye.

Anne's eyes widened. Why had the Marquess of Crewe's handsome face flashed into her mind? With a wooden expression on her face, she answered, "No."

Lady Jersey, with quick perception, pounced on Anne's reluctant demeanor. "Ah, but you're shamming us, my dear. How delightful. I love romances! Who's the lucky gentleman?"

Anne turned a pointed shoulder to her inquiries. "I don't know whom you're talking about, Lady Jersey."

Lady Byrne frowned at this. "She's talking about you, Anne," she explained, shaking her head at Anne's denseness.

"No, I'm not. I'm talking about the fellow who has obviously won Lady Anne's heart. Who is he?" Lady Jersey demanded.

At that moment, Reeth entered the salon and announced the Marquess of Crewe. Anne was so startled that she jumped guiltily. Lady Jersey clapped her hands with glee, obviously not needing a more blatant hint than a woman's nearly jumping out of her skin at the mention of a man's name.

She wagged a bony finger at Anne. "Sits the wind in that corner?" she cried. "Oh, you naughty puss. I daresay you see a resemblance of your late husband in him. How romantic." She clasped her hands and sighed.

Anne, who had not yet detected any resemblance between the two brothers but was still determined to try to do so, merely shook her head in confused annoyance.

Lady Jersey beamed, while Lady Byrne eyed Anne with suspicion. "But I thought," the duchess began darkly, "that you and he didn't rub along well together. I distinctly recall that last night—"

Anne hastily cut her off, chagrined, with an embarrassed cough, looking at the doorway. "Never mind that, Aunt Honoria. He's here."

And he was. He sauntered into the room looking bang up to the knocker in a riding outfit of the first elegance. His buckskins were skintight and showed off to advantage his muscular thighs. His drab coat was well cut, the points of his shirt collar were starched, and he sported a Belcher tie. His dark hair was arranged in the Bedford style, and he held in his strong grasp a beaver hat and a pair of tan gloves.

Even Lady Jersey was awed into silence at the sight of him. Anne found her voice first. "To what do we owe the honor of this visit, my lord?"

He raised a supercilious eyebrow and directed his gaze to his aunt. "I would like to request permission to take your niece for a ride in Hyde Park. I suggest you have the groom saddle the bay hack. It's a docile mount and will not afford Lady Anne any undue discomfort."

"If you think I need a docile mount, you're fair and far off indeed, my lord," Anne fired back, bristling at the aspersions cast on her riding skill.

He ignored this interpolation. "And in the meanwhile, Lady Anne can run upstairs and change her dress."

Anne seethed with anger at this high-handed treatment, but knowing Lady Jersey was observing her closely and with the liveliest curiosity, she refrained from snapping at Crewe. If Lady Jersey thought she nursed a *tendre* for this infuriating gentleman, she couldn't be expected to rip up at him, could she? So instead, she swallowed her resentment and smiled prettily up at him. He was startled, but he quickly regained self-control and maintained an impassive rigidity as Anne shyly and with a batting of her eyelashes told him she would be ready in a trice.

Lady Jersey was heard to give a sigh of satisfaction. When she made her farewells to Anne, preparing to bring her morning visit to a close, she gave Anne a conspiratorial wink. And Anne was able to soothe her lacerated emotions with the knowledge that she had succeeded in her gambit. It would not be long before the latest *on-dit* would be raging through the town: The new heiress had lost her heart to the Marquess of Crewe.

Anne wondered if Pastor Max would be put out at hearing his name on everyone's tongue. As she hurried up the stairs to her bedchamber, she devoutly hoped so.

She set her new abigail, Lucy, in a bustle to lay out her riding dress, and soon Anne descended the stairs attired in this wonder. It was an outfit of blue velvet with a high-standing collar heavily trimmed with lace, narrow lace ruffles at the wrist and a waterfall of a muslin cravat. Blue kid gloves and half boots and a tall-crowned hat like a shako with a peak over the eyes and a plume of curled ostrich feathers were the suit's accessories.

The Marquess of Crewe eyed this dashing outfit with evident disapproval. "You can't go out dressed like that. You'll be the cynosure of all eyes," he exclaimed.

Lady Byrne hurried to the defense of her protégée. "She's so beautiful, she'd be the cynosure of all eyes no matter what she wore."

"Even if I wore nothing," Anne murmured outrageously.

Max drew in an angry breath. "Especially if you wore nothing!" he almost shouted, causing Lady Byrne to start at his vehemence.

"Really, Max," she tut-tutted, "I don't know what you're making such a fuss and rumpus about. It's not too dashing for Anne. She is a widow, you know."

"And how I know."

Anne waited tensely to hear him denounce her to his aunt, declaring that she had made herself a widow by sending Simon to his grave, but for some inscrutable reason, he refrained. Relief made her put up her chin. "Yes, remember? I'm the wicked widow."

"Really?" huffed Lady Byrne, upset at this injustice. "I wouldn't go so far as to say that. If you were to go about wearing nothing at all, now that would be wicked, but there's nothing exceptionable in a riding suit of such undeniable modishness!"

Max stared at Lady Byrne for a perilous moment, then burst out laughing, much to Anne's surprise. She stared at him in wonderment. Well. He certainly looked pleasant when he smiled, didn't he? The dark expression on his face lightened, and his gray eyes gleamed. But as the marquess quickly recovered his gravity and turned quite coldly to Anne, her cordial feelings toward him vanished.

"We don't wish to keep the horses standing, do we?" she asked demurely, challenging him to object again.

"No," he said, capitulating abruptly, no doubt bored with the discussion of riding outfits.

Anne kissed Lady Byrne on the cheek and exited through the door held imperiously open for her by Max.

Once she was outside, her eyes opened wide with sincere admiration at the sight of Crewe's black as it was led up to its owner.

"That's a prime bit of blood, that is," she declared with twinkling eyes.

His expression softened. Obviously he was proud of his mount. "I'm happy to have met with the wicked widow's approval," he said with an attempt at irony.

"Are you?" She looked skeptical. "But it's not you who've met with my approval; it's your horse."

His mouth twitched in acknowledgment, and she skipped up to the saddled bay held ready for her. She petted its soft muzzle. "What a lovely creature," she cooed. "What's her name? I wish I had thought to bring some sugar lumps with me."

"Her name's Bolster," the marquess informed her impassively. "I hope we are not going to stand around here talking and wasting the entire afternoon."

Anne darted a look at him, closed her mouth in a tight line and mounted without the assistance of the groom. Unlike Crewe's horse, which he mounted, hers gave her no trouble by dancing and sidling nervously about but, rather, lived up to its duly descriptive name. She nodded, and the two silently set off toward St. James's Street, quickly reaching the wrought-iron gates that led into Hyde Park.

It was the fashionable hour, and the park was well frequented by members of the ton. Spanking chaises, phaetons and barouches wheeled sedately down the lanes lined with poplars and statues. Lone riders on hacks dallying with pretty ladies who peeped up from underneath frivolous parasols and strollers giving themselves a gentle airing on the promenade all enlivened the scene before Anne.

"We shall make a round down Rotten Row and give the passersby a chance to view the new heiress," Crewe informed her as they trotted along. "It will do your reputation good to be seen with me."

Her mouth dropped. Of all the pompous statements! "I hope it will improve your reputation to be seen with me, Pastor Max," she said through gritted teeth.

He ignored her, merely nodding austerely at a passing curricle.

"Just why did you ask me to accompany you today for a ride in the park?" she asked suddenly.

"Because I had no doubt that if I did not, you would set off in the company of some ineligible suitor or, worse, by yourself, and do everything in your power to become a byword in the town."

She flung a look at his profile. It was hard and graven. Lord, the fellow was inhuman. "I never thought that you would take such an interest in me," she said in a dangerous voice.

Crewe stopped to give greetings to a Lady Fairford who was bowling along in her open chaise, the monstrous ostrich feathers on her bonnet waving like flags. Anne forced herself to smile and be agreeable but was relieved when they continued on their way.

"I do not care about you," Max said now, as though their conversation had not been interrupted, "but I do care about my family's reputation."

Anne nodded in sudden understanding. "How foolish of me to forget. True, I wouldn't even be here in London if you weren't so concerned with your family's reputation."

Max obviously felt this statement needed no response, for he gave none.

"But what's a family, anyway?" Anne asked in an indifferent voice. "Simon told me about your family. You have scores of cousins, all of whom you consider to be mere acquaintances and whom you barely see except on special occasions. A couple of married sisters, each engrossed in her own concerns. A mother whom Simon described as a silly wigeon, and a father whom Simon called an insufferable tyrant. How can you really care about people like that?" she demanded, putting her hand on her hip.

"I was bred to care about people like that," he snapped, jabbing at his reins and causing his horse to rear slightly. He controlled the horse immediately with his strong hands. He looked at her a little contemptuously. "I was born to be a marquess, my lady. That may have little meaning to you, but I was inculcated from the day of my birth with the responsibilities and duties this position would hold for me. One of the first considerations is always to uphold the honor of the family."

"It's a pity Simon didn't set such store by the honor of your family," she muttered, almost to herself.

Crewe stared at her with an arrested expression on his face, his eyes narrowed. "What did you say?"

She shook herself and gave a fatuous smile. "I said nothing at all. What a pompous little boy you must have been, so aware of your position in life."

He was silent for a long moment; he seemed to be brooding. "I was taught to be aware of my position in life," he said finally, patting his horse's neck absently. "Lord, I was constantly surrounded by nursemaids, governesses, tutors, servants—all of them at my beck and call. All of them making very sure I kept to my exalted station in life. Even my friends were chosen for me by my parents for fear I would take up with someone unworthy of me. And my leisure activities were chosen for me by my parents for the very same reason."

Anne started to say, "How docile you must have been," then stopped, realizing how overpowering it must have been for a small boy to have been supervised so carefully. His natural spirits must have been nearly stifled. She looked at Max with new eyes. No wonder he was so pompous and stuffy.

"They couldn't have chosen *all* your leisure activities," she pointed out. "Especially as you got older," she said, with a significant look.

His mouth twisted. "By leisure activities, I suppose you mean women."

She was taken aback by his bluntness. "Well, women are considered a major concern for most men," she said reasonably. "Why didn't you arrange a life of your own? One would think you'd have felt you owed it to your family to marry quickly and set up a nursery. Haven't you ever found a woman that you could lo—uh, marry?"

"A woman I could love?" Max finished, with a disdainful lift to his eyebrow. "I had not thought to find the wicked widow so idealistic."

He did not say more, and Anne, unable to help herself, prodded. "But have you never lost your heart?"

"I've had ample opportunity to do so. Gad, I've had women throwing themselves at my head for as long as I can remember." He shuddered.

"And you never met one you wished to marry?"

"Marry?" Pastor Max was clearly astonished. "Lord, I'm inclined to consider women more as children to whom I would rather give a sugar plum than my time. Forsooth, they are the greatest barrier to matrimony I know."

Anne burst out laughing. She wiped her eyes, then tightened her hold on her horse's reins. She almost went off again at the disdainful look Pastor Max was giving her. "My goodness, Pastor Max, I pity the woman you ever do marry."

His mouth tightened. "Oh, you do, do you?" His nose went up. "I think any woman blessed with my offer of marriage would be grateful."

"You have it wrong there, my lord. It would be all the *other* women who would be grateful."

"I suppose I could return the compliment," he said grimly. "And with more reason."

He was obviously thinking of Simon and the misery she had supposedly put him through. All the laughter died out of her, and she stared at Max for a tense moment. Then she managed a wry smile. "You delight in setting up my back, don't you? Well, I shall not gratify you by flying up into the boughs." She turned her head away, pointedly ignoring him.

Her pleasure in the ride through the park was completely cut up. Once again she was depressed and furious, and it was very difficult to ride beside him with even the semblance of composure. But she forced herself to do so. She smiled and greeted a number of entities traveling Rotten Row. Max made a point of bringing her to the attention of all the more commanding personalities of the ton, such as the Princess Esterházy, who rode in great state in a large carriage with a driver before and a tiger behind. The princess smiled graciously at Anne, congratulating her on her meteoric success.

"Everyone's in raptures for you, dear," she drawled, tipping her handsome head.

Anne raised an ironic brow, contemplating Max. Everyone?

She held conversations with a number of personages whom she had met at the rout the night before. All seemed eager to pigeonhole the latest heiress, ready to gossip and chat and win her interest.

But Anne was not interested. She chafed to be away from the marquess. He was insufferable. How dare he lead her about as though she were a puppet? She was just about to suggest they leave the park when her eyes widened at a most unusual sight.

Lord Sherringham was honoring Hyde Park with his presence. He was being driven in a high-perch phaeton pulled by a team of grays. He was lolling on the cushions, his legs straight out before him, with his head resting on the squabs. His heavy weight caused his side of the carriage to tilt so drastically that the phaeton looked woefully lopsided. Ninian and Stanhope were riding in his wake.

"Oh, look," Anne exclaimed. "There's Sherringham."

"You needn't shout out that information, my lady. He would be nearly impossible to miss," Max drawled.

She motioned to the group, and Ninian and Stanhope promptly pulled up their hacks and headed toward her.

"What a delight it is to see you again, Lady Anne," Ninian declared with boyish enthusiasm. Stanhope was obviously glad to see her as well but seemed incapable of stating this fact out loud, although he did manage to smile shyly at her.

"No more glad than I am to see you. Pastor Max is a most tedious conversationalist," she explained, looking at Crewe from under her eyelashes.

"But what's the use of talking when you're riding?" Ninian demanded. He eyed her horse with disfavor. "It's hard to tell that you are riding, Lady Anne, if you'll forgive me for saying so. I've never seen such a lamentable hack." He shook his head disparagingly. "Looks long in the wind."

Anne took affront at this criticism. "Let me tell you that I'm such a tearing rider, Lord Wainfleet, that I could make any horse look like a Thoroughbred."

"Oh, is that so?" hooted Ninian, gathering his reins, ready to do battle.

Anne was just about to spur her horse into a furious gallop when Max's hands clamped down over her reins. She lurched forward but held her seat. "What the devil are you doing?" she gasped.

His mouth twitched at her strong language, but he said coldly, "One does not gallop in Hyde Park."

"Oh, I forgot!" Ninian cried, looking perfectly white and aghast at his near slip. "It's not at all the thing." Anne looked questioningly at Geoffrey Stanhope, and he nodded gravely.

She looked at Max, a dangerous expression on her face. "You're taking too much after your father, my lord. You may like playing the tyrant, but I refuse to submit to you. You may not want me to gallop, but just try to stop me!" And with that, she wheeled her bay about and let it have its head down the stretch of tan that lay beside the carriage road.

"Hell and the devil!" Ninian cried, and set off in hot pursuit, waving his hat wildly. Max and Stanhope set off, too, and Anne could hear the pounding of a veritable cavalcade behind her.

Exhilarated, she urged her horse forward until it fairly flew. She hoped Max was feeling duly angry. She might have kept this pace up for quite a time, but unfortunately she glanced behind her shoulder and was so much struck by the sight of the mob tearing after her that she was thrown into the whoops and perforce drew her horse up at the end of the path. She leaned over the pommel, panting and laughing.

Max was the first upon her, soon followed by Ninian and Stanhope, and he looked thunderous. His mouth opened to deliver her a terrific scold, but Anne, convulsed with laughter, stopped him with a feeble gesture, pointing at Sherringham's phaeton, which was surging along drunkenly after them. Apparently he had told his driver to spring 'em, and the carriage was swaying violently back and forth, forcing Sherringham to clutch at the sides. He was perspiring and looked so ridiculous that Max stared openmouthed and then burst out laughing.

The phaeton stopped beside them. Sherringham struggled to catch his breath and asked weakly, "Are you all right?"

Max, the smile still on his lips, said, "I was just about to ask you that question, Sherringham. Have you a maggot in your skull? What induced you to race about in that neck-or-nothing manner? You'll probably have to take to your bed for a week."

"Two weeks!" he gasped. He swallowed and asked his driver to fan him with his beaver hat. "I thought Lady Anne had lost control of her horse. Was coming to the rescue."

This response set all four of them into the whoops. Sherringham was not Anne's idea of a knight in shining armor. Far from it. And the idea of Sherringham playing Sir Galahad was exquisitely humorous. She blinked and shook her head. "Oh, Sherringham, how wonderful you are, willing to sacrifice yourself in that way for me."

Sherringham, put out by their merriment, huffed, "Yes, I thought it was rather wonderful. I only hope

I have not permanently damaged my constitution. As it is, I'm starving." He turned his head to his driver. "Home!"

His driver flicked the leaders, and Sherringham, without saying another word, took his leave of them.

"I never saw such a sight," Ninian gasped, still laughing.

"And I hope you never do again," Max said severely. He rounded on Anne. "Lady Severne, I think you've done enough damage for one day. I'm taking you home!"

She bridled at his imperious tone but decided it would be wisest to follow him without argument. She nodded a dignified farewell to Ninian and Geoffrey Stanhope and then set off behind the marquess. Her resentment soon evaporated, however, and she was filled with unholy glee at the number of censorious glances that were cast at the Marquess of Crewe as he made his way out of the park. So it really was a social gaffe to gallop in the park! Mrs. Drummond-Burrell, to Anne's delight, even stopped her carriage and clucked furiously at their retreating forms. Anne had scored!

Her triumph enabled her to be gracious to the marquess. He led her into the nearest room at Byrne House and delivered himself of a thundering scold, which Anne sat through without protest.

The marquess, quite unused to such docility on Anne's part, quickly found the wind taken out of his sails. He said, in a much milder tone, "I daresay you are unused to London ways. I shall just have to keep a closer watch on you."

Somehow this prospect did not fill Anne with dismay. Without meaning to do so, she smiled at him.

"Well, I know that you will always do what you think best. Pastor Max," she added, unable to resist teasing him a little.

His dark eyes flashed, but he refused to rise to the bait, merely admonishing in a cold voice, "Just mind your manners at Almack's, Lady Anne."

Anne was surprised. "Are you going to be there?"

He looked grim. "You may be sure of it. You don't think I'm going to turn you loose at Almack's on your own, do you?" He shook his head pityingly. "You must be all about in your head."

And on that pleasant note, he left.

Anne put her hand to her chin and reviewed the events of the morning. She was well on her way to luring Max into some outrageous scandal. She hadn't thought it possible that such a correct gentleman could exist in the world. And to think it was Simon's brother. The difference in the brothers' characters was marvelous indeed.

Odd how personalities reveal themselves. The late marquess, Max and Simon's father, had been something of a tyrant. Max had deferred to his father's wishes and had grown into a perfect—almost too perfect—marquess. Whereas Simon had been regardless of his father's wishes, hell-bent on burning out a shameful path for himself, even going so far as to marry out of hand a little country nobody just to spite his father, who had desired Simon to marry an eligible heiress already picked out for him.

It was a lowering realization to think that Simon had never really loved her, even from the beginning. She shook herself. *Don't think of the past,* she admonished herself. But wasn't it odd how completely blind to his brother's true character Max was?

He probably did not wish to admit to himself that anyone of Severne blood could be a rakeshame.

Her mental meanderings were interrupted by Reeth, who informed her that the duchess wished to see her.

"So there you are, my dear." The duchess smiled upon Anne's entrance into the drawing room. "There was something I most particularly wished to say to you."

"Yes, aunt?"

"Yes." She nodded and gave Anne a grave look. "Do you feel mentally prepared to make your entrance into Almack's tonight?"

Anne looked a little nonplussed, and her mouth opened in surprise. Mentally prepared?

Lady Byrne gave a knowing nod. "Yes, I knew it would be so." Her face became grim. "Why everyone looks forward to Almack's as unalleviated entertainment I'll never know. It quite daunts me."

"Does it really?" Anne asked in lively dismay.

"To be sure," the duchess asseverated. "I find it most arduous to remember all their rules and regulations. You mustn't arrive a moment after ten, or you will be denied admittance. You must not dance the waltz without the express permission of one of the patronesses."

"Is there anything you *are* allowed to do?"

"Why, of course! You may flirt to your heart's content, and you may dance until dawn. It is expected that all young people should take advantage of the marriage mart."

"This prospect does not compensate for their strict regulations. I can see that it must cast quite a damper on one's pleasure to behave always in form."

"It's not that, precisely." The duchess frowned. "It's just the necessity of remembering all the strictures that puts me all on end."

Anne strove to keep her countenance. "You poor dear. Well, we shall just have to support each other." She patted the lady's hand soothingly.

Lady Byrne gave her a grateful smile. "You are a treasure, my dear. That reminds me. You must wear your simplest gown. It need not be white, of course, but it should be something quite demure, very correct. They won't let you in if they don't think you look at all the thing."

Anne blinked in surprise. "Are they so particular that they even lay down requirements for dress, Aunt Honoria?"

She flung up her hands. "So particular? You idiotic darling. Of course they are particular. They're particular about everything, and that is why Almack's is so important." She gave a tiny shrug and said with unwonted worldliness, "I daresay if Almack's were haphazard with its rules and requirements, everyone would find it a dead bore and no one would care to go there above half. As it is, everyone dies to go."

Anne started to deny that she was dying to go, but then she stopped. Oh, yes, she was dying to go. Hadn't the Marquess of Crewe announced his intention of attending the assemblies to keep an eye on her? Well, he had best keep an eye on himself.

"I shall do everything you say, Aunt Honoria. I have no desire to put you to the blush." She couldn't repress a wicked chuckle. No desire to put Aunt Honoria to the blush. Only Pastor Max!

Lady Byrne patted her on the cheek and advised her to take herself off to bed to rest up for the evening's exertions.

Anne, having just promised to do everything her aunt advised, was forced to smile feebly in acquiescence and to retire wide awake to her bedchamber.

Once ensconced under an eiderdown, however, she must have dropped off into a doze, for she was quite startled when the abigail flung back the bed curtains a few hours later. Anne sat up in bed and took the cup of hot chocolate held out to her. Then she prepared herself for the evening ahead.

The dress she was helped into was a gown of azure-blue sarcenet, with an ivory body, tiny puff sleeves of lace and seed pearls, and cut low across the bosom. It was a simple, delicate confection, and she looked extremely fetching in it. A pretty sapphire pendant was suspended on a gold chain round her white throat. Blue satin slippers, long gloves and a fan of frosted crepe on ivory sticks completed her toilette.

Lady Byrne found nothing to condemn in her looks and promptly bustled her into a waiting carriage, allowing Anne only a cursory view of her own costume. The duchess was attired in an emerald grosgrain-and-velvet gown and sported the famous Byrne emeralds, which consisted of a tiara, a necklet and an elaborate corsage.

"We must not be late," the duchess reminded her as they settled into the vehicle, which set off at a brisk trot for King's Street and the wonderful Almack's.

Once arrived, Anne was granted leisure to survey her surroundings. She did so and could barely repress a snort of disgust. Why, there was nothing wonderful about the place at all. The music was passable, to be sure, and the dancing pretty, but the rooms were not overly splendid, and the refreshments, well, they were paltry indeed. Bread and butter, cake, lemon juice, tea and orgeat. Tidbits, merely. Passing the gaming rooms, she saw that a few tables were indeed set up, but since the gambling was confined to shillings play, only dowagers and old doddering fathers filled them.

Obviously, Almack's attraction was as a suitable background for the splendid and beautiful presence of the London ton. And so she observed them a moment. There were a number of lords, earls and dukes in attendance, most of whom were simply ogling the young ladies. A number of dowagers were reclining in chairs against the wall, including the stern Mrs. Drummond-Burrell. They were all no doubt censuring some innocent young debutante's behavior. Lord Cyprian Denzil caught Anne's eye for a moment, for he was wearing a costume all of gold, and his heels, which were preposterously high, glittered with diamonds. Breathtaking. But because she considered the man himself far from breathtaking, she quickly turned away. Finding nothing of real interest to catch her eye, she sighed, feeling rather flat.

All feelings of disappointment in the place, however, vanished when Lady Jersey fluttered up to them. She was wearing an evening gown of dull yellow brocade. "He must be mad about you, dear!" she exclaimed without preamble.

Both Lady Byrne and Anne stared at her, startled. "Who?" they demanded in one voice.

"Why, the Marquess of Crewe, of course. Who else?"

Anne was too stunned to speak.

The Duchess of Byrne, rarely too stunned to speak, scoffed, "My dear, you must have windmills in your head. I don't think Max even likes Anne."

Lady Jersey dismissed this attempt at humor with a wave of her bejeweled hand. "Mere subterfuge. You can't fool me. His attentions are too pointed."

"What can you mean?" Lady Byrne demanded.

"Why, he hasn't attended the assemblies at Almack's for years. But," Lady Jersey declared in portentous accents, "he's here tonight! And all because Lady Anne is here."

"Well, there's nothing wonderful in that," sputtered Lady Byrne. "He's here to please me. He's a very good nephew. As a matter of fact, the best of nephews. I've often been beholden to him for some kind act on his part. Don't you remember the time he hired that house for me in Brighton, when I had been assured there were none to be had? And when he emptied his greenhouse to fill my ballroom with flowers only because I said I might fancy to try a new type of decoration? And—"

Lady Jersey interrupted her. She had no patience to sit through a catalog of all of Max's wonderful doings. "I'm positive he must be bewitched by Anne. However did you do it?"

Anne, not wishful of disabusing Lady Jersey of her illusions, merely shrugged. Lady Byrne stared at her, astonished.

Her astonishment redoubled when Lady Sefton, a very pretty lady with corn-gold hair and china-blue eyes, led the Marquess of Crewe up to them. "Such a popular young lady you are," she said in her soft voice. "I've been besieged by requests for your hand in the waltz." She cast a coy look up at Max, who looked particularly impassive. "I felt your brother-in-law held precedence, so may I offer him to you as a partner?"

Indeed, the notes of a waltz were being struck up, and Anne demurely put her hand on the marquess's arm and allowed him to lead her out to the floor. Lady Byrne gave an audible gasp, and Lady Jersey fell to whispering in Lady Sefton's ear.

Anne suppressed her amusement and studied Lord Crewe. He was looking his usual sartorial self, dressed to perfection in black satin knee breeches, a white waistcoat, striped stockings and a waisted coat with very long tails. He was unadorned by any jewelry, his black hair was styled in the Windswept, and he was undoubtedly the most elegant gentleman in the room.

His expression was austere, and his lids drooped over his dark gray eyes, making him look a disdainful partner. He was, however, a graceful dancer, moving with the ease of an athlete. Very aware of his strong arm placed around her waist, Anne said carefully, "You dance very well."

"I know."

Her eyes twinkled at this abrupt reply. He was holding himself on too high a form. "I am honored you deemed me a suitable partner for the waltz," she said in a deceptively shy voice.

"I would never deem you a suitable anything, my lady," he said coolly. "You are outrageous. I chose to dance with you merely to remind you that you are being kept under close scrutiny."

She gave him a roguish grin, which caused him to blink at her. "We couldn't get closer than this, could we?" She sighed, fluttering her eyelashes.

He glowered at her and closed his lips in a firm line. Anne waited hopefully for a more audible response, but he gave none. He was a most unsatisfactory partner.

"How is Lord Sherringham?" she inquired audaciously, forcibly reminding him of her earlier indiscretion in the park.

"He is as well as can be expected," Max answered shortly.

"Why is he not here tonight?" she persevered.

His mouth twisted in amusement. "Sherringham never attends Almack's. You must know he never dances!"

Anne could feel the force of his logic and gave a small chuckle. "I wonder what he is doing this evening," she said in a fond tone.

"Probably poring over his magnificent objets d'art," Max said wistfully.

Her eyebrows shot up. "You wish you were with him?"

"But of course," he declared, with a look of contempt. Obviously anything was preferable to standing up for a waltz with her! "I would be able to ask him his opinion of a new Tintoretto I've purchased. It's an exquisite painting."

Anne gave a polite smile. Art was interesting, to be sure. But not while one was dancing. She knew Max was quite a connoisseur, so she said, with an attempt at good manners, "How fortunate for you to have found a Tintoretto. Are you certain it's not a sham?"

He looked down his very straight nose at her, his lips curling. "Of course I am. I know what's a fake and what isn't."

His words very nearly surprised a bubble of laughter from her. "You do, do you?" she asked ruefully, having no great personal confidence in his self-declared clarity of judgment.

He obviously did not feel it necessary to defend himself, for he merely stared at her with suddenly narrowed eyes. He seemed to be studying her intently, and for some reason she found her face growing hot.

She abruptly turned her head, surveying the other occupants of the room, trying to appear nonchalant. Max followed her lead and soon started frowning. After a few moments he said indignantly, "Do you know, we're being closely observed by quite a number of people. I wonder why?"

Upon looking around, she realized he was correct. They were apparently the center of attention. Anne could have enlightened him as to the reason for this had she chosen. Lady Jersey, no doubt, had been doing her work with a will. Anne was hard put not to laugh.

"Oh, are we?" she replied indifferently, after a pause. "I daresay you've set everyone on their ears by attending the assemblies tonight."

His nose wrinkled. "I find it very distasteful."

She started to murmur "What a pity," then was suddenly assailed by an idea of how to make it even more distasteful for him. Her face was very still for a moment as she looked up at the marquess. They danced a few bars in silence.

Then, "Oh, my," she gasped, passing a shaking hand over her forehead. "I feel very strange." And without further ado, she collapsed against his chest in a dead faint.

"What the devil!" he ejaculated, missing a step and almost colliding with another couple. He clutched Anne frantically to him as he quickly regained his balance. He gripped her arms tightly, trying to hold her upright. Anne's head lolled back and then forward as he gave her a light shake.

"Of all the damned things," he muttered.

Anne's mouth twitched with mischievous pleasure. She could barely suppress her merriment. She forced herself to remain limp, however, resting her cheek against his surprisingly broad and strong chest. She was enjoying this.

The marquess went rigid, and suddenly Anne yelped with pain. He had administered a sharp pinch to her arm, and her eyes flew open involuntarily as her hand covered the hurt.

"Why in God's name did you do that?" she demanded, in a surprisingly vigorous voice for one just recovered from a fainting spell.

He swept her into the waltz once more. His eyes gleamed, and he looked decidedly smug as he said, "Why, I couldn't think of what else to do, my lady, there being no water handy to fling in your face!"

She stiffened with outrage. "You wouldn't dare."

"On the contrary, I would have felt quite compelled to do so."

"You're monstrous," she burst out, fuming.

"I was going to say the same of you. Do you always faint while you're waltzing? It must be awfully inconvenient."

She bit her lip. "It was the heat," she said vaguely. He chuckled, and she gave him a burning glance.

"Yes." He nodded, enjoying her discomfiture. "I can feel it."

The fellow was intolerable! "I'm tired. Take me off the floor," she demanded tersely.

His hand tightened painfully over hers. "When the dance is finished." He looked down at her pityingly. "What did you think I'd do when you fainted? Cause an uproar by carrying you off the floor?"

That was exactly what she had hoped he would do, and the fact that he had outsmarted her put her out immensely. "I would never expect you to do the gentlemanly thing," she flashed.

"I thought it was extremely gentlemanly of me to resist the temptation of holding you helpless in my arms," he said pensively.

Anne was so surprised she nearly stumbled. He caught her up and rebalanced her by pulling her so close to his chest that it took her breath away.

"Are—are you flirting with me?" she gasped.

"No." His eyes glinted down at her. "Just making certain you don't 'faint' again."

Well, thought Anne, clamping her mouth shut and seething with indignation, he would soon learn his mistake if he thought he had got the better of her!

CHAPTER FIVE

THE NEXT DAY Anne did not know whether to be gratified or diverted when Lord Sherringham paid her a morning visit.

Lady Byrne had no such doubts, for she exclaimed with pleasure and hurried forward as he ponderously seated himself on the yellow sofa in the drawing room. He breathed heavily for a few moments at the exertion; then his hanging cheeks creased in a pleasant smile. "How glad I am to find you both at home. I would have been appalled to have made the journey to your house only to find you out."

"It would have been ghastly," Lady Byrne agreed, not the least satirically. "We decided to rest up after our triumphant night at Almack's. Else, I daresay, I would have taken Anne to Kensington Gardens for a promenade. Or to Somerset House to see the Elgin Marbles. Though I'm not sure she would have enjoyed seeing them, being all broken up as they are. I don't see how anyone can cherish a statue of a woman that doesn't have a head. It's absurd, don't you think? I mean, it's almost an insult to womanhood. As though we don't have heads. I daresay we're frippery creatures but not precisely mindless," she declared with feeling.

Sherringham, who had gone into such raptures at the sight of the beautiful Greek statues from the

Parthenon that he had had to be carried out of Somerset House on a chair, merely smiled.

"We missed you at Almack's," Anne said quickly before Lady Byrne could catch her breath. "I hope you weren't indisposed by your morning's misadventures in Hyde Park."

"Oh, no," Sherringham replied comfortably. "I took to my bed and administered to myself with bowls of thin gruel. They made me feel so done up that I took myself off to Watier's, where I passed a very pleasant evening." He smacked his lips in toothsome memory. "But how flattering to think you noticed my absence." He bowed slightly. "I'm afraid I could never go to a waltzing ball."

"I quite understand."

He shifted his massive weight with difficulty. "But I do intend to attend Prinny's ball at Carlton House tonight. I hear you were sent an invitation?" It was a question.

"Yes, indeed," Lady Byrne averred. "And such handsome invitation cards they are, with their flourishing print and gilt edges. Prinny knows just how to do things up right."

Reeth came in with a tray of refreshments, and Sherringham waited to be handed a glass of ratafia. "Vile stuff," he murmured, swallowing it carefully. "But it's too early to have anything stronger. And as to Prinny's ability to do things up right, I'm not quite so certain. His tastes are a little too extravagant for me." He pondered a moment, pursing his fat lips. "As a matter of fact, *he's* a little too extravagant for me."

Lady Byrne was not shocked at this criticism, knowing that the Prince Regent and Sherringham were the best of friends and that Sherringham was on such easy terms with Prinny that he could venture a disparaging statement with impunity. The two had many things in common, not the least of which was their corpulence.

Sherringham turned his head slowly toward Anne. "I came to inquire what you intend to wear at Carlton House this evening."

Instead of being put out, Lady Byrne, answering for Anne, expressed great pleasure at his condescension. "You did?" she clapped her hands. "Why, how very kind of you to take an interest. It's not every woman who can avail herself of your advice in matters of dress."

"Quite true." Sherringham accepted her raptures imperturbably.

Lady Byrne put her finger to her lips. "I wonder if I should have Tilly bring the gown down. No, I'll describe it to you."

"Please do."

"It's a gold crepe, trimmed with blond lace and worn over a satin slip."

"And how will her hair be dressed?" he asked, his brow wrinkling with concentration.

"A la Titus."

He nodded slowly. "You should confine the cluster of curls with a simple gold ribbon."

Lady Byrne nodded, listening to his strictures avidly.

"Will she be wearing jewelry?"

"I was going to lend her my topaz necklet."

He winced and swallowed convulsively. "No, no," he said weakly. "Really, you mustn't. It would not be at all the thing. Diamonds."

Lady Byrne flung up her hands. "Why, of course! Why didn't I think of it? I have the perfect set. A necklace, brooch and bracelet."

He lifted an admonishing finger. "Earrings."

Lady Byrne's mouth dropped. "Just earrings? Don't you think that rather paltry?"

"No. I think it subtle. Unlike the prince."

Lady Byrne let his words sink in. "I see." She nodded. "Well, I agree that would be the very thing."

"Fine. And I shall present Lady Anne to the Prince Regent."

Lady Byrne gasped. "No! Really? How very kind of you. It will make her!"

"I suppose it shall," he acknowledged stolidly. "You may not like the prince, Lady Anne, but I promised Max I would make you known to him."

Now it was Anne's turn to gasp. "You promised Max?"

Lady Byrne tittered with pleasure, preening herself. "Max is a darling. The best of nephews. We must be sure to thank him tonight."

Anne had not yet overcome her resentment of Max from the previous night. He was the worst of brothers-in-law, as far as she was concerned. The most complete hand. A regular old squeeze crab. It put her into a stew just to think about him.

Sherringham must have seen her darkling look, for he said, "Is Max in your black books, Lady Anne? It seems to me that you are displeased with him."

She couldn't trust herself to open her mouth, so she said nothing.

He tilted his head, his brows lowering. "Very odd. For Max seems to be taking a most unusual interest in you. Most unusual." Anne was not in the least flattered by this information, but she refrained from saying so, while he was silent a moment. "Does he remind you of your late husband?" he asked.

Anne was so much revolted by the comparison that she almost cried "No!" Then she checked herself, and in a more subdued tone, said, "Max is not at all like Simon." At least not yet.

"Do you like Max?"

"I dislike him excessively," she said, a little too hotly.

"Very odd." He was observing her carefully, though lazily. "I don't think Max likes you, either. But you both seem mightily interested in each other, nevertheless."

Anne shrugged her shoulders airily.

Sherringham sighed and began to struggle up from his seat. Both Lady Byrne and Anne hastened to assist him. As they reached the door, he turned slightly and gave her a piercing glance as he asked, "Did you like your husband?"

He did not miss the telltale blush that crept into her cheeks. Anne was fortunately not obliged to answer because Lady Byrne exclaimed, "What a ridiculous question, Sherringham. She was married to him, wasn't she?"

"Just so." And he left them.

What an odd visit that was. Unfortunately, it was not the last. Sherringham's departure was followed by the appearance of Lord Epworth, one of Anne's more determined admirers. He was impervious to such snubs as abstracted attention, yawns and sighs, finding it impossible to credit that anyone, least of all a woman honored with his favored address, could find him dull. He chatted desultorily and with a drawling voice upon a great number of subjects, and Anne couldn't help but let her mind wander to more interesting subjects, the most engrossing being my lord Crewe.

So, he had induced Sherringham to take her under his aegis. She wondered why. Probably so she'd feel obligated to him. Well, she refused to feel obligated to him. He was impossible. The stiff-rumped prude. She was determined to do something to rock him out of his self-assured complacency. She quite thought she had had him last night. But, instead, it had been she who had been put out of countenance. Obviously, Pastor Max was an opponent worthy of her steel. How anyone so intelligent could be so stupid she had no idea. She had every intention of opening his eyes—at least to his own faults—at the first opportunity. She would have to see what could be contrived at Carlton House.

She was recalled to her surroundings by Lord Epworth, who coyly demanded her opinion of a snuffbox he had purchased. It was of Battersea enamel and rather too frivolously decorated for Anne's taste.

"I think it suitable for afternoon wear, don't you?" He sighed, serene in the conviction that his tastes were shared. "Lord Petersham brought it to my attention. Vastly obliging of him."

"Vastly." And she watched with a jaundiced eye as he took from his pocket a tiny silver shovel with which to scoop the snuff. All the crack, or so he hastened to tell her. Lord, he was a coxcomb. Anne suddenly found herself wishing for Max's company. He wouldn't countenance this worthless fribble. He would deliver himself of a scathing and well-phrased setdown, sending Lord Epworth to the rightabout without further ado. No matter how infuriating Max was, he was not paltry. And he was far more interesting than this Lord Epworth, and anyone else she'd ever met, for that matter.

Finally ridding herself of Epworth's unwanted presence, Anne was able to devote herself to preparations for her appearance at Carlton House. She soaked luxuriously in a hip bath scented with ambergris. Then she reposed on a sofa, after a light repast of fruit and tea, for an hour or so, an application of the Lotion of the Ladies of Denmark upon her face.

By evening she was attired according to Sherringham's prescriptions and found herself quite pleased with the result.

But standing in front of Carlton House at the hour of the ball, next to Lady Byrne, Anne decided that her appearance might well go unnoticed in comparison with the fantastic beauty of the structure before them. She had heard much of Carlton House from the duchess, who had described its seemingly countless rooms in exhaustive detail. Lady Byrne had not exaggerated. It was a spectacular pleasure-dome palace.

Prinny had gone greatly into debt building Carlton House and, staring at its fine Corinthian portico, built by Henry Holland, which gleamed with classical dignity, Anne felt wholeheartedly that the expense had been well worth it.

Prinny had thrown all caution to the winds as he gathered expensive treasures with which to adorn his palace. Pictures, girandoles, clocks, looking glasses, bronzes, Sèvres china, Gobelin tapestries and countless other treasures were brought to London by agents of the prince—one of whom was Max himself, so Lady Byrne said. Cabinets, chests and tables built by Riesener, Weisweiler and Carlin; marble busts by

Coysevox; bronzes by Keller; candelabra by Thomire; pictures by Pater, Vernet and Greuze were all bought and placed tastefully within the palace. Prinny was sorely lacking in many qualities expected in a prince, what with his extravagance and scandalous love affairs, but his taste in the visual arts must surely redeem him to all critics.

Carlton House looked to be extremely crowded with guests that evening, but this was only natural. Prinny's parties were always horrible crushes, and because he refused to open any windows because of a deadly fear of fresh air, his guests were made highly uncomfortable, stifling in an overwhelming heat. But of course, the discomfort was as naught. One was in Carlton House, the very center of the beau ton, and Prinny's guests braved the stuffiness of the house for the pleasure of being there. Anne felt a cold excitement in her breast as she entered the splendid entrance hall, with its Ionic columns of brown Siena marble, leading to a huge octagonal room with a graceful double staircase.

Lady Byrne pressed Anne's hand and gave her an encouraging smile. She headed Anne toward the reception line, hoping to make her greetings to the prince, but it was discovered that he was not stationed there to greet them. She admonished Anne not to get into the fidgets; they could place their dependence on Lord Sherringham. Then they were announced, in stentorian accents, by a dignified footman.

They made their way to the ballroom, and Anne blinked with awe at the magnificent room. Its walls flashed with gilded mirrors reflecting the huge shining chandeliers suspended from the painted ceiling. It was filled to overflowing with twirling dancers who glittered and sparkled with color and gaiety. She took a deep breath, not quite believing her eyes. It was all so beautiful. It must be a dream.

But no, it was not a dream, for there, near the end of the ballroom, separated from all the other most respectful guests and dancers, was the Pastor Max with Lord Sherringham, both of whom were attending a portly gentleman with a florid complexion. The large gentleman was shaking his head and appeared to be weeping copiously.

Egad, that must be Prinny. She gaped at him a moment, but quickly regained her poise when she found herself being pointed out to the prince by Lord Sherringham. Then she caught hold of Lady Byrne's hand for support as she realized that, after a moment of heavy scrutiny, the prince was wending his way toward them, with Lord Sherringham.

Although the room was crowded, his progress was not in the least hampered; the dancers moved out of the way as if by magic. Without giving anyone else the slightest glance, he made straight for Anne and Lady Byrne.

Anne couldn't help but cast a triumphant glance about her at all the other occupants of the ballroom. Here she was, a perfect nobody, about to be greeted by the Prince Regent. She was, indeed, a success.

Lord Sherringham waited a suspenseful moment to catch his breath. Then he said simply, "Your Highness, I wish to introduce you to Max's sister-in-law, the Lady Anne Severne. I think the sight of her beauty will give you pleasure."

Prinny was almost entirely hidden from view by Lord Sherringham's girth. He stepped from behind this gentleman, blinked and leaned forward suddenly. His hand went to straighten his fair hair, and he seemed quite taken by the sight before him.

Anne, however, was far from taken. The prince was fatter even than Sherringham. And, unlike Sherringham, he did not have the elegance of taste to hide the defects of his figure by avoiding any extravagances of fashion. In fact, he was the most gaudily dressed gentleman she had ever seen. He was wearing a velvet suit of a dark color with emerald stripes, superbly embroidered down the front and seams with a wide border of silver flowers mingled with fiery diamonds. His waistcoat was of white-and-silver tissue embroidered like the coat. His garter ribbon was fastened with a shoulder knot of diamonds, and on his chest glittered a profusion of stars and orders.

Even Lady Byrne was struck silent by the sight of him.

He held out his pudgy hand to Anne. "You are a widow?" he inquired with something perilously close to a leer. Anne curtsied and gingerly shook his hand. Much to her discomfiture, he squeezed it significantly. She felt herself turn beet-red, uncomfortably aware that Max had joined them.

"Y-yes, Your H-highness," she stammered. "I am a-a widow."

"The wicked widow," Lord Crewe murmured irrepressibly.

The prince looked highly pleased with this information, actually licking his lips. "Wicked, eh?" His plucked eyebrows waggled. "I think you and I must have much in common. Perhaps you will join me in this waltz, and we can discuss it."

Anne nearly froze with terror. Unconsciously, she cast an imploring look of entreaty to Lord Crewe. He stared at her for an inscrutable moment, then stepped forward.

"Your Highness, I'm afraid Lady Severne has an aversion to the waltz. It makes her faint." His face was expressionless, but Anne knew he was laughing at her. She did not care in the least. She was too thankful to him for rescuing her.

He held out his arm to her, and she almost clutched at it. "I've promised to show her your conservatory, my prince. I hope you will excuse us."

The prince began to protest, but since Lady Byrne quickly endorsed this scheme, he was left with nothing to say.

And so Pastor Max swept the wicked widow away.

Anne let out a sigh of heartfelt relief as they departed from the ballroom, actually pleased to be in Pastor Max's unalarming hands. There was something to be said for prudish ways, after all. At this moment, she preferred to be with Max more than with anyone else in the world. Max heard her sigh and looked down at her with a queer smile on his lips. "I had not thought to find you so missish," he commented maliciously.

Her eyes flashed, and she put up her chin. "I'm nothing of the sort. He just..." She groped for words, then shrugged. "He just overwhelmed me, that's all."

"He's notoriously overwhelming."

"If that was so, I find it amazing that you took such trouble to bring me to his notice," she said angrily.

They came upon a cluster of celebrants in the large hallway, and Crewe was obliged to slow his pace so they could make their greetings. As they continued forward, he said in a cool voice, "Nothing in my experience with you led me to believe that you would take exception to the prince's amorous manners."

Her hand itched to slap his face. "Well, I'm afraid you have a mistaken notion of my character," she exclaimed before she could stop herself. Then she checked herself and pressed her lips together resolutely.

"Apparently that is true," he said thoughtfully. "I would never have expected you to be thrown into a virgin panic. Actually, it was most diverting."

"Of course, you would find it so," she replied in frigid tones. She no longer felt in charity with him and wished that he would go away and leave her alone. "You are insufferable, and I have no wish to keep company with you."

He retained his grasp on her arm. "What, willing to brave the lion? Prinny is still on the loose, my lady. I would not care for him to set you up as his latest flirt, so please oblige me by staying at my side."

"I have no intention, as you so delicately put it, of being set up as Prinny's latest flirt. Or anyone else's, I might add," she flashed, looking him militantly in the eye.

"So you do have some notions of propriety. How intriguing. I wonder if Simon knew of this side of your character."

"Of course he knew," she snapped, then broke off in consternation. His dark brows lowered, and he frowned at her. She tried to regain ground by saying, "And he knew just how to tease me out of my strait-laced ways."

"He did, did he?"

There was a harsh note in his voice that she didn't like. But even less did she like to talk about Simon. "Let's speak of something else, if you please," she said hurriedly.

His mouth became hard. "Still wearing the willow for your husband," he observed. Nothing in his frowning aspect led her to believe he was pleased with this observation. "Well, no doubt you can have recourse to your diary with all its store of pleasant memories for solace."

Her eyes dropped to the floor. "No doubt," she said in a stifled voice.

She waited meekly for him to say something cutting about her and her diary, but he didn't. Then she plucked up. What a goose she was, waiting meekly for him to say anything to her. She refused to be meek with this man. He was toplofty enough without her bowing to him. No matter what he thought of her, and he certainly thought the worst, she had done nothing wrong in her life—not to him or Simon. Of course, it could be said that her blackmailing him into allowing her to come to London by threatening to publish her diary was a reprehensible action. But she comforted herself with the thought that the money spent for her Season was her own. And she could spend it any way she chose to. Actually, she thought her use of her inheritance was quite commendable—to reform Pastor Max from his stiff-necked ways. And she would continue trying to do so.

She took a deep breath. "Where are Ninian and Mr. Stanhope?" she inquired.

"In the gaming room, I've no doubt."

She brightened perceptibly. "Really? Well, let us join them by all means."

"We shall join them by no means," he replied inexorably.

She stopped. "Why, how perfectly ungracious. You couldn't deny me the pleasure of seeing them again. It would be thought most rude of you."

"By whom?"

"By me!"

"You can think me a damned rudesby for all I care. I have no intention of leading you, a female, into the gaming room."

Her eyes widened in comprehension, and she snorted. "Oh, is that all? What scruples you have." She dismissed them with a wave of her hand.

"You seem to have some, too," he reminded her. "Prinny."

"How naggy you are. I told you, he just overwhelmed me. I was not prepared for such condescension on his part." She said this in as earnest and as sincere a tone as she could muster.

"How modest you are. Prinny always has a soft spot for beautiful ladies."

She gaped at him. "For what?"

"For beautiful ladies," he replied imperturbably.

She felt a blush rising in her cheeks. "You think I'm beautiful?"

He gave her a contemptuous glance. "I hold with the maxim that beauty is only skin-deep. Prinny, however, does not."

How perfectly ungallant he was. It nearly made her blood boil. She opened her mouth to give a hot rejoinder; then she closed it. It would be useless to pull caps with him. It would lead to nothing. "Why not take me to the gaming room?" she asked after a short pause. She gave a saucy grin. "We could engage in a card duel. I'll make the stakes worth your while."

His eyes swept over her body in a far from contemptuous manner. "What would you put up?"

"My diary?" she ventured.

He laughed. "You almost tempt me. Almost, but not quite. I'm afraid I'm not a gambling man. I don't trust myself to fortune."

"How stolid you are. Most prudent. I daresay your parents squeezed all your frivolity out of you while you were still in your long coats." She shook her head sadly. "What a pity."

His nose went up. "I think they did well."

She laughed at that. "Of course you would. But you know, there is a happy medium to attain between your stodgy prudishness and Simon's—" She caught herself up. She was certainly letting her tongue wag tonight.

"You were saying?" he asked quietly. His eyes seemed to be boring into hers, and she swung her gaze away, giving a light shrug.

"Oh, that I can understand your hesitation, that's all. Some people are so leery of losing. I have no such qualms. So, if Ninian and Stanhope are deep in a game, I shall endeavor to join them."

"Not while I have you in hand, you won't."

"But you don't have me in hand," she declared, and started to pull away, but he tugged her to him with such violence that she collided against his chest. He held her close for one breathtaking moment, their faces almost touching. She could only stare at his burning eyes, as though mesmerized.

After a moment, she bethought herself and pushed him away, breathing hard. She was quite ruffled and felt considerably annoyed at herself for being thrown into such a flutter. "Really, my lord, you are becoming positively brutish. Some women might be delighted by such an exhibition of manly strength, but I am not."

His lips curled. "My dear lady, you exaggerate. If you think that small display an exhibition of manly strength, you should see me at Jackson's Sparring Saloon."

He looked so complacent that she longed to give him a set-down. "Don't tell me you box," she said in an incredulous tone.

"Yes, of course I do. The Fancy's quite a proper sport." He gave a supercilious lift of his brow.

Proper. How she hated that word. She allowed a coquettish glint to flash in her eye as she surveyed his muscular form. "I wager you would strip to advantage," she murmured, pretending to drink in his masculine beauty.

He went rigid with shock. "How dare you say such a lewd and improper thing!" he gasped.

This was more than she could bear. "Don't look so shocked, my lord," she admonished playfully, though through gritted teeth. "You must know that everything I say—or do—is improper!" And with this Parthian shot, she swept away.

She stalked into the nearest room, seething. It was the Chinese salon, and it flickered with hundreds of butterfly lanterns. With its pagodas and Chinese statuettes it looked most exotic, but Anne was in no mood to admire its beauty. *Damn Pastor Max,* she thought, pacing angrily about. She couldn't abide him. She stopped in front of a porcelain sage with pendulous earlobes. She'd show him, she told the statuette; then she stopped short, giving a wry smile. She was being foolish beyond permission. This was certainly not the place to show anyone anything. She must go back to the ballroom.

She returned to this glittering wonder and was immediately accosted by a number of gentlemen begging her hand for the next dance. Lord Epworth was most importunate, holding out his beringed hand to her. She almost took it but her glance caught a most felicitous sight. Ninian and Mr. Stanhope were leaning against the wall, and Ninian was motioning violently for her to join them. She gave her excuses to the gentlemen surrounding her and made her way toward them.

"I thought you were in the gaming room," she said.

Ninian didn't answer her. He was eyeing her disappointed suitors with amusement. He thumbed his nose at Lord Epworth and then turned to Anne. "Lord, what a lot of silly bucks you have hanging out for you. None of them do you justice, you know."

"What a handsome thing to say." She laughed. "I am most flattered."

"Truth," put in Mr. Stanhope. Anne curtsied to him in acknowledgment, causing him to turn red.

"Why aren't you in the gaming room?" she inquired again. "It's so unusual seeing you on the dance floor."

"We were in the gaming room and in the middle of a damned good game of cards, too, I might add. But Prinny came in."

Anne looked to Mr. Stanhope, and he nodded and gave a shudder. She turned back to Ninian's boyish countenance. "Did he ask you to leave?" she demanded.

"Oh, no. We didn't leave. We fled. He was foxed, you see. He always gets this way when he has a set-to with someone."

"Does he?" Her eyes widened. "Tell me about it."

Ninian laughed, shaking his head. "He's really quite a character. Usually, after a serious quarrel, he succumbs to violent fevers for which he is severely bled. And then—" he warmed to his task, enjoying having an avid listener "—to offset the debilitating effects of the bleeding, he drinks great quantities of wine, and when wine fails to produce the desired effect, he tries liqueurs of every description. He becomes a regular roaring-boy before the night ends."

Anne was duly impressed. "My goodness. I think it was very wise of you to take to your heels and run upon sight of him."

Ninian looked pleased with her approval. "We thought so, too. But now we're condemned to the ballroom, which is not my notion of an interesting place to be."

She could well believe him. She murmured her commiseration, trying to suppress a giggle.

"Aye, you may well." He accepted her spurious sympathy with a darkling eye. "But it's worse than you think. Stanhope's been cast into the mopes, and all because of Denzil."

She made a grimace of distaste. "What, is he here?"

Ninian nodded grimly, indicating a thin gentleman engaged in a waltz with a very pretty young dab of a girl. He was dressed in a pink coat. His collar points were outrageously high, threatening to poke out his eyes; he had a monstrous cravat, and his hair, arranged in artful disorder, glistened with pomade. It was enough to turn one's stomach. Denzil, unlike

Max, was a gentleman who reminded Anne forcibly of her late husband, a circumstance that did nothing to recommend him to her.

"Mr. Stanhope doesn't like Lord Denzil?" she inquired.

Ninian shook his head, his arms crossing over his spare chest. "No, nor do I. He's not at all the thing," he explained. "As a matter of fact, I'd be more than happy to thrust a spoke in his wheel."

"Too ramshackle for my taste," suddenly averred the usually inarticulate Geoffrey Stanhope.

Anne was ready to agree with both their judgments, though she was rather surprised to hear Mr. Stanhope actually state his. She followed Lord Denzil's progress on the floor. He danced in a mincing style that quite set her teeth on edge, and he was whispering in the ear of his obviously discomposed young partner.

"Who's that pretty little chit he's intimidating?" she asked.

"Amy Farlow," declared Stanhope, in a burst of eloquence.

Anne eyed him speculatively. "She seems a nice girl," she ventured.

"Wonderful!" he burst out, with great feeling.

Anne eyed him now in the liveliest curiosity. "Mr. Stanhope, do you know her well?"

This direct question reduced poor Mr. Stanhope to stammering incoherence.

"She's a good girl," supplied Ninian. "But her parents are a couple of vultures. The Farlows are as poor as church mice, and they have three daughters to marry off. They've actually thrown poor Amy to Lord Denzil."

Anne was revolted. The poor girl was obviously terrified of the man. And she had good reason to be. He was an ugly customer with a reprehensible reputation. He was known by all, so Lady Byrne had told her, to be a consummate libertine. It was cruel of her parents to put her in Denzil's way. "How perfectly horrid," she exclaimed. "It's cradle snatching!"

Mr. Stanhope, fully in agreement with these statements, nodded gloomily.

"I take it, Mr. Stanhope, that you cherish a *tendre* for this young lady," she hazarded.

Mr. Stanhope was quite unable to reply.

"Of course he does, the gudgeon," Ninian declared.

"Well, why don't you cut Denzil out?" Anne demanded. "You're just as eligible as he is."

Mr. Stanhope shook his head in excruciating embarrassment. "Don't have his address," he replied in stifled tones, staring longingly at his Amy.

"True," Ninian seconded. "Stanhope's no good at all with the ladies. Denzil, however, has quite a way with them."

"Yes." Anne nodded, remembering with distaste her first meeting with him. "He's a shocking flirt." She tilted her head and stared intently at Mr. Stanhope's miserable countenance. Her heart went out to him, the poor fellow. And out to poor Amy Farlow, too. "Well," she said purposefully, "something must be done about it. If you won't cut Denzil out, I must contrive to cut out Amy."

Mr. Stanhope goggled at her.

"Oh, the wicked widow's on the warpath," exclaimed Ninian, giving a war whoop and executing a neat step, his exuberance causing Anne to laugh out loud.

Her laughter subsided as she watched Denzil with calculating eyes. "I don't think I shall have too much trouble gaining his interest. I can be an outrageous flirt, too."

"Outrageous is the right word!" Ninian laughed gleefully.

Mr. Stanhope stepped forward and wrung her hand gratefully. "Wonderful."

The set finished and Denzil prepared to take Miss Farlow to her mama, who was stationed in a bergère chair along the wall. Anne took Stanhope's arm and gave it a twitch. "Intercept them, Stanhope! Ask her if she would care for a glass of lemonade or something."

His eyes started out in sheer horror at the audacity of such a plan. He started stuttering some craven words, which Anne effectually cut off by propelling him forward with her hand at the small of his back.

"Don't be in such a taking. We haven't a moment to lose. I shall be right behind you," she assured him.

They hastened forward, and as Stanhope clumsily accosted Miss Farlow, Anne walked straight into Lord Denzil with a resounding bump.

"Oh, my goodness gracious," she gasped, stepping back. Lord Denzil swayed on his feet from the impact but did not lose his balance. He started to swear in exasperation, then stopped when he saw who his pretty bumper was.

His face became immediately wreathed in smiles, and he swept a low bow to Anne. "A thousand pardons, my dear lady. I hope I did you no harm."

She put her hand to her bosom as though to calm a palpitating heart. "Dear me, no," she managed in a weak voice.

"Unpardonable clumsiness on my part," he lied gallantly, eyeing her white bosom. "My only excuse is that I was dazzled by your beauty and was unable to see my way clearly."

"Oh, la, my lord." She tittered, giving him a tap on the arm with her fan. "Very prettily said."

His eyes became intent and his nostrils quivered. "All speeches made to you must be pretty, my lady, if only to match their recipient." He smirked, and Anne was hard put not to roll her eyes in disgust and make a quick escape.

He started to turn suddenly, as though having remembered Miss Farlow. Anne, desperate, quickly pinched his cheek, not wanting him to see that Miss Farlow was in Stanhope's hands. He nearly jumped at this coquetry, so surprised was he, but Anne only smiled innocently up at him. "My lord, you're putting me to the blush." She batted her eyelashes so, he stared at her, fascinated.

Anne's mind was busily working away, though her expression did not betray this fact. Should she lure Denzil into some private tête-à-tête, or should she just dance with him once or twice?

Her speculations were interrupted by the timely entrance into the ballroom of the Prince Regent. He was as drunk as a wheelbarrow and almost exploded into the room.

Within minutes, he set the entire place into an uproar by posting himself at the doorway, to the terror of everybody that went by. The first victim was the Duchess of Ancaster, who had no sooner entered than

Prinny flung his arms about her neck and kissed her with a resounding smack. The poor lady shrieked and fled incontinently from the room.

Anne's eyes became round as saucers as she watched in amazement as Prinny accosted old Lord Galloway. He whipped the wig from this poor gentleman's head and threatened to knock out his false teeth.

The prince looked just like an actor on the stage playing all the pranks of a drunken character.

Deciding to take advantage of this unusual situation, Anne clutched Lord Denzil's hand in fright. "Oh, Lord Denzil," she cried. "Please take me away. How terrifying this is."

Denzil's thin chest swelled, and his eyes gleamed as he patted her hand reassuringly. "Have no fear, Lady Anne, I will protect you. But you're right. We should leave immediately. I know a quiet place."

Anne was certain he did. She was almost sorry to let herself be led out of the room, for there was bound to be quite a show. Prinny's flunkies, dressed in their green-and-yellow livery, were starting to circle warily around the prince, trying to decide just how to overset him. But, she thought with a sigh, she could not fail Mr. Stanhope.

Without hesitation, Denzil led her through a bewildering number of apartments, up the grand stairway and through several saloons and antechambers. He did not stop to greet any acquaintances, and Anne soon found herself in the conservatory, feeling hot and out of breath.

The conservatory was a magnificent structure of glazed glass, filigree, statues and gauze, but she did not stand to admire it, her only thought being to find a chair in which to sit down.

She was not so dead to her purpose, though, that she forgot to choose a chair well screened from view and intimate. She sank onto a bench behind a statue of a reclining Venus. Lord Denzil sat down beside her. Very close beside her. He retained his grasp on her hand, and Anne had to steel herself not to snatch it away. She clutched the fan she held in her other hand.

"How ecstatic I am to be given this chance to be private with you, Lady Anne," he breathed, holding his face so close to hers that she could see that he rouged his cheeks.

She suppressed a shudder of revulsion. "Oh, are you? I can't think why."

His breathing became slightly labored. "No? I'll tell you why. Any man would be ecstatic at having the opportunity to be private with you."

She turned her face away slightly. "But you're not just any man, are you, my lord?" she managed.

He inched even closer to her, and she found herself involuntarily leaning backward. "Don't tell me I'm even the slightest mite special to you, Lady Anne," he cried, transferring his grasp from her hand to her upper arms.

Anne opened her mouth to give some shy disclaimer but instead gave a sudden shriek and nearly fell off the bench when a furious voice shouted behind her, "What the devil are you doing?"

She tore herself away from Lord Denzil, who was too paralyzed by shock to move. Then she cast a surreptitious glance upward. It was, of course, Pastor Max.

CHAPTER SIX

LORD DENZIL, succumbing to a craven impulse, bent and retrieved Anne's fan, which she had dropped upon being startled by Lord Crewe.

"Please allow me," he gasped, handing her the fan, bowing to Lord Crewe and then beating a hasty retreat from the room—all in one swift motion.

Anne followed his retreating form with rising indignation. Of all the shuffling fellows. She would take him to task for this, leaving her at the mercy of my lord Crewe.

Swallowing with a little difficulty because of a suddenly constricted throat, she turned to Lord Crewe and managed a feeble smile.

"Did you wish to see me, my lord?"

He seemed to be towering over her, and it was obvious that he was exercising the greatest restraint to keep himself from wringing her neck. "No, I did not wish to see you, my lady. I felt it my duty to find you, and it was a damn good thing I did. I turn my back for one second, and you immediately embark upon some indiscretion."

She sniffed, plucking up her courage. "Why did you feel it your duty to find me, my lord?" she asked in a conversational tone.

His teeth ground together. "Because Prinny has gone on the rampage, and I thought to spare your being confronted by him in such a state by taking you home.''

She stood up readily. "I'd be happy to return home, my lord. This party has fallen sadly flat, I'm afraid.''

He pushed her back on the bench with the palm of his hand. "You must first tell me what you were doing with Lord Denzil,'' he declared in an ominous tone.

Her eyes kindled indignantly. "What do you think I was doing with Lord Denzil?'' she demanded, in such a self-righteous tone that he was startled into being defensive.

"I don't have to think," he snapped. "I know. You were embracing!'' He divulged this in accents of shocked outrage.

"How do you know he wasn't helping me recover from a faint?'' she asked, staring him straight in the eye and putting up her chin.

He looked a little disconcerted but stuck to his guns. "I know you, my lady. That's enough to convince me you were embracing.''

"Oh, I was forgetting that you know me so perfectly well,'' she said in a completely unabashed tone. "I suppose you thought embracing was the most I could be doing in so public a place. How forbearing of you.''

"Do you know what type of fellow Lord Denzil is?'' he flashed, reverting to taking the offensive, his face belligerently close to hers.

"I'm not certain, so you must tell me,'' she said sweetly. "All I know is that for some indefinable reason, he reminds me of my late husband, Simon.''

Lord Crewe was so taken aback by this revelation that he stared at her agape. He couldn't trust himself to speak for some appreciable length of time. Finally he burst out, "How dare you compare my brother with that damned rakehell?" His face was absolutely livid.

She was surprised at his vehemence. "I didn't compare them at all, my lord," she pointed out kindly. "I just said that Denzil reminded me of Simon. That being the case, you must know that I couldn't resist him."

He looked revolted. "Are you telling me you're attracted to Denzil?"

She gave him a coy glance. "I'm always attracted to some man or other."

"Your levity, my lady, is most unbecoming!" he said with asperity. "I think you must not realize to the full the extent of the impropriety you have committed."

"I fear you are right. You must tell me." She disposed herself to listen to him with an air of great interest.

He looked at her with dislike. Taking a deep breath and forcing himself to unclench his fists, he began, pompously, "It would be thought most improper for you to be seen holding a tête-à-tête with a gentleman. Especially someone of Denzil's reputation."

"But I'm holding a tête-à-tête with you, my lord," she pointed out, her eyes wide.

"I don't have Denzil's reputation!" he refuted with violence.

She shrugged and took his hand, pulling him down close beside her. "I can contrive to overlook that," she murmured, her eyes smiling significantly into his.

He stared at her for a breathless moment, his face a study in fascinated horror. He actually started to lean toward her before he caught himself up, flushing. He shook himself and achieved a mocking smile. "I don't believe I've ever had such a palpable lure cast at me before," he observed with due impress.

"Never?" she repeated commiseratingly. She patted his hand. "Poor fellow. You have led a dull life, haven't you?"

His mouth twitched as though he had to bite back a surprised laugh. "No, you vixen," he returned. "Just a *proper* life."

She nodded. "Ah, yes. I was forgetting that. Proper." She put a finger to her chin. "You may call yourself proper, my lord, but I still call you dull. Do you never do anything for mere entertainment?"

He considered her words with a seriousness that surprised her. "I find diversion in art, and in horses and in clothes."

"All superficial amusements, my lord," she quickly pointed out. "You should find diversion in human beings. Though we are not perfect, as is art, we are at least real."

He gave her an amused smile, his dark eyes narrowed. "Well, I never thought to find you such a profound philosopher. I'm sure you have had so great an acquaintance with human foibles that you could easily teach me how to be diverted by them."

"I could teach you many things."

His lips curled unpleasantly, and Anne realized with mortification that he must have been leading her on. "Assuredly, my dear Lady Anne. How to be a confirmed rake, for instance."

"I would find that a most interesting task," she said as evenly as she could, through gritted teeth. "And most unnecessary. Lord Denzil, already being a confirmed rake, offers greater possibilities."

His superior air left him, and he quickly descended into glowering ire. "You're not to see Denzil again!" he commanded, clenching his fist.

She was unimpressed. "Of course not," she agreed. "At least not when you're so near at hand that you can interrupt us."

His mouth clamped shut. His chest swelled with seething anger. She had every expectation of seeing him explode. But he disappointed her. He controlled himself with a superhuman effort and flung out his hand to her imperiously. "We shall leave this place at once!"

She was disappointed at this abrupt curtailment of their tête-à-tête. She had hoped to enrage Max so greatly that he would have been forced to try to strangle her. Attacking his sister-in-law would have plunged him into just the sort of scandal she wished for him. But she comforted herself with the thought that at least she was alive and able to try again the next day.

She sighed and placed her hand on his proffered arm. "How sorry I am to leave this place. I was becoming excessively fond of it. Especially of all the nude statues placed about."

He emitted a choking sound, but he vouchsafed no answer, merely marching her out of the conservatory. He promptly collected Lady Byrne, overriding her expressed desire to remain a few moments longer. Prinny was still performing in the ballroom, and she was sorry to miss the fun. Max, however, was in no mood to be amused by Prinny's drunken antics and led Anne and Lady Byrne resolutely out to the portico, where he immediately set off a linkboy to call for their carriage.

This equipage turned up the drive, and Max handed his aunt and Anne into it. The postilion put up the steps and closed the door, and Max signaled the driver to be off, still not having uttered another word to Anne.

Lady Byrne made up for his deficiency, for she uttered many words during their drive home.

"My, what a vastly diverting ball, was it not?" Lady Byrne queried, looking out the window and still in the highest of spirits. "Prinny can be so comical. I daresay he was a trifle foxed tonight. That is the only explanation for his behavior. Unless, of course, he's touched in his upper works, which isn't all that impossible, you know. His father," she declared, in portentous accents. "I've heard that King George has been seen talking to trees, of all things. Poor fellow. He must be past praying for." She paused, considering. "I once talked for a great length of time to a chair. But the person who had occupied it left without my knowledge, so I believe there is some excuse for me."

Yes, and also for the person who had sneaked away to escape her lengthy monologue, Anne thought to herself, smiling.

Lady Byrne continued chatting on as the carriage rattled home. Upon entering the house, Anne kissed her fondly on the cheek and said a hurried good-night.

She was not in such raptures about the Carlton House ball as Lady Byrne had been. It had, actually, presented quite a problem: Lord Denzil. The man turned her stomach, and she knew she was courting danger by encouraging him. But Mr. Stanhope, in his inhibited fashion, was courting his dear Miss Farlow. And he must be allowed to do so without fear of competition from Denzil. Mr. Stanhope was the type

of fellow who needed all the encouragement in the
world to express his feelings to another, and if he
found himself rivaled by any gentleman, let alone the
flirtatious Lord Denzil, he would be rendered incapable of even catching his lady's eye.

So Anne was determined instead to catch Lord
Denzil's eye, but to be wary of him. She had made a
fairly promising foray into this project before being
surprised by Lord Crewe. And she had no doubt that
Denzil would be one of her first morning callers the
next day.

And as for Pastor Max, he was more than living up
to his name. She was more and more determined to
show him up for his cruel treatment of her, but first
she would have to handle Lord Denzil.

THE NEXT MORNING, Denzil was indeed an early
caller. Anne and Lady Byrne received him in the
drawing room. Anne proceeded to flatter and to tease
him into the greatest good humor, a not untrying task,
for he was dressed most idiotically in a riding outfit of
canary yellow. He was also perfumed. He hung upon
Anne's words, ogling her, winking at her and smiling
so significantly at her that she was hard put to it not
to slap his face. Instead, she asked him to take her out
driving in the park.

His painted mouth screwed up, hesitantly. "Oh, ah,
my dear, really," he hemmed. Obviously, he had designated poor Miss Farlow for this very public treat and
was loath to change his plans.

Anne pouted. "It's such a lovely day, and I would
so love to take an airing."

He pulled abstractedly at his lace cravat, and Anne
almost turned away in exasperation, but she caught

herself up, thinking of poor Miss Farlow's fate if she failed. She decided to cajole him. "And I've heard so much about your driving skill, my lord." She sighed. "I've had an ambition to ride with you for this age. I can just imagine how strong and able you must look. It sets my heart in a flutter."

Lady Byrne, whose attention had been wandering during much of this visit, caught these words and gave Anne a hard stare. "Are you feeling a trifle out of sorts, dear? Your heart is in a flutter, did you say? You must be as sick as a cushion."

Anne was understandably put out by this interruption. She hurried into speech. "Oh, Aunt Honoria, how amusing you are. You quite take my breath away." She giggled and rolled her eyes. Denzil joined her and laughed so heartily that he was obliged to take a heavily scented lace handkerchief from his sleeve to wipe his eyes.

Lady Byrne stared at the two of them, obviously considering them candidates for Bedlam. At her expression, Anne couldn't help but laugh in earnest.

When Denzil could speak evenly, he stood up and held out his arm to Anne. She forced herself to stand and take his proffered arm. "I would be most honored," Denzil said in a simpering voice, "to take you for a ride in the park, Lady Anne."

"How excessively obliging of you," she murmured.

HYDE PARK, which only days before had seemed a pleasant enough place, was now turned into a scene of terror and fright. For Denzil, as a driver, left much to be desired. In fact, he was downright lethal. He was lamentably cow-handed and had a tendency to lose control of his leaders. To make matters worse, he chose to drive a high-perch phaeton, a vehicle with huge hind wheels and a body fully five feet from the ground. Risky enough when driven by a man with the greatest skill, it was a vehicle of heart-stopping danger when driven by Lord Denzil. After a few minutes of being rocked abominably, tilted and rattled quite out of her temper, Anne knew that all was lost. She would be dead before the afternoon was through.

Denzil, happily oblivious of the reason for Anne's green face, bowled along at a great pace, narrowly missing a tree or two, and pulling up, with difficulty, to give greetings to several passing acquaintances.

The fact that Anne was willing to risk her life to be with Lord Denzil in his carriage must have given these acquaintances an exaggerated view of her attachment to him. Lady Jersey, in her open barouche, veering to escape Denzil's headlong approach, looked astonished at seeing Anne with him.

Denzil plumed himself on all the attention he aroused and turned toward Anne, saying with effulgent warmth, "Lady Anne, you have no idea the pleasure it gives me to be in your company."

She begged him, terror-stricken, to keep his eye on the horses.

He giggled as he, thankfully, did her bidding. "It is most difficult to do so. You are a far more pleasant sight than all these trees and carriage houses. So pleasant a sight that I am forced to beg you to allow it to me again—tomorrow night, to be specific."

Anne followed his speech with difficulty. "I beg your pardon?"

"Oh." He tittered. "I hope I am not being too forward. I beg of you to join me in a visit to the Pantheon Masquerade tomorrow evening."

Anne frowned at his words. The Pantheon Masquerade. She wanted to flirt with Lord Denzil, but she was no fool. The Pantheon Masquerade was notorious for the wanton behavior of the masqueraders. All kinds of people attended it, all intent upon having a veritable revel-rout. She would attend no such place in Lord Denzil's company.

"But aren't masks worn to the masquerade?" she inquired after a moment.

He blinked at her vapidly. "Yes, I think so. Else they wouldn't be called masquerades!" He gave a shrill peal of laughter at his own witticism.

Anne managed a perfunctory smile. "Well, if I'm wearing a mask, how can you be afforded another pleasant sight of me?" she asked.

Her reasoning was so unanswerable as to render him speechless. Anne smiled to herself, pleased with having dealt with him so effectively, and turned her attention to the riders on Rotten Row.

A spanking high-perch phaeton driven by a regular top-of-the-trees sawyer caught her eye. It was Pastor Max.

Denzil saw Max also and was preparing to halt. As these preparations included flicking his leaders with a careless whip, Anne closed her eyes and clutched apprehensively at his arm. "Please, please don't stop," she hissed, imagining a sickening collision. "I-I do so enjoy being private with you."

Denzil complied with her wishes, giving her a great wink, and so it was seen by all that the wicked widow had given the Marquess of Crewe a cut-direct!

Anne knew she had raised seething conjecture when she caught Max's expression. He looked mad as fire. She comforted her conscience with the realization that she had just saved him from being wrecked into splinters, and so she shrugged and tried to forget the incident.

The ride continued interminably, but Anne was not killed. She was inordinately happy to be conveyed back to Byrne House to find Lady Byrne and Lady Jersey waiting for her.

Denzil bade her a lingering good day, kissing her hand tenderly and holding her eyes with his. He walked backward through the door, his eyes still on hers, until Reeth, prosaically, slammed the door in his face.

Anne hurried to her room to change her clothes, and stepped into the salon in time for tea. Lady Byrne poured a cup for Lady Jersey. Anne seated herself gracefully on the settee beside Lady Byrne, taking up a raspberry tart, and started munching away.

Lady Jersey turned to her and wagged a bony finger at Anne's nose. Anne stopped chewing and blinked at it. "What a naughty puss you are," she chided the astonished Anne.

"I beg your pardon?"

"I saw you in the park with Denzil," Lady Jersey declared. "You naughty, naughty girl."

Lady Byrne looked flabbergasted. "What do you mean?" she demanded in a querulous voice. She looked at Anne, fear in her face. "Don't tell me Denzil made improper advances to you in the park of all places and you accepted them."

"Of course not," Anne denied, revolted.

Lady Byrne heaved a great sigh. "Oh, thank heaven." She gave an uncertain laugh. "I don't know why I thought you did, except, of course, you weren't feeling quite well when you left, and I thought he might have taken unfair advantage of your weakness. He's just the sort of fellow who would, you know."

Anne nodded in agreement, an action Lady Jersey was quick to catch. "See? You are a naughty puss. Using Denzil in that reprehensible way. You deserve to be beaten, my girl." Since her eyes were dancing with amusement, Anne was relieved to realize she was teasing.

"I don't understand you at all," Anne declared, reaching for a plum cake.

"I wager you do, my girl," she answered. "I saw the way you cut Max in the park."

Again Lady Byrne looked flabbergasted. "What a terrible thing to do, Anne! I can't believe it of you. And after he's been so kind to you. To cut Max." She stopped and tilted her head. "I wonder how you did it. Did he bleed profusely?"

Anne choked on her cake. She managed to shake her head.

Lady Jersey chose to mount her high horse. She said, in an austere tone, "I see you wish to make game of me."

Lady Byrne was quick to deny it. "That thought never entered my head, I swear. Few thoughts do, actually. For I wouldn't even know how to go about it. Some people are good at making game of others, but I'm no good at all. I always feel like crying if I hurt someone. And how can a joke be any good if it makes you feel like crying, I ask you?"

Her reasoning was so profound that Lady Jersey could think of nothing to say. For at least two seconds. "Well, that's by the by." She turned to Anne. "You needn't think you're fooling anyone, dear. I'm awake on all suits, and it's pretty obvious to me that you're using Denzil to make Max jealous!"

Anne, perfectly entranced with this view of her actions, sighed with delight.

Lady Jersey gave a crow of laughter. "See, I knew it," she cried in gleeful triumph, swallowing a plum cake whole. "You deserve to be beaten, my girl, just as I've said."

"Those are my sentiments exactly," a voice from the doorway informed them.

All turned in surprise to see that Lord Crewe had just entered the room. Lady Byrne flew out of her chair to greet him. Under cover of the commotion she made, Lady Jersey gave Anne a huge wink and whispered, "See? It's working already. He looks as cross as crabs."

Anne tried to appear duly gratified by this observation. But it was difficult. Max certainly did look cross. His brow was thunderous, and though he exchanged pleasantries with his aunt, Anne could see that he was laboring under a furious temper.

When Lady Byrne invited Max to be seated, he declined, instead looking directly at Anne and saying, in an ominous way, "I would like to speak with Lady Severne in private, if you please."

His tone was biting. Although his face was perfectly expressionless, it was obvious that he wished to rake Anne down.

She put up her chin. "For what purpose, my lord? To give me a bear-garden jaw?"

He gave her a particularly humorless smile. "You won't know until we are in private, will you?"

Lady Jersey, agog with curiosity, gave Anne a little nudge. "Go on, dear. Lady Byrne and I can have a comfortable coze, so you mustn't stay here on my account."

Anne expressed herself as vastly obliged to the woman. With a resigned air, she rose from the settee and led the way to the yellow salon, a small room that looked out on the back garden. It was furnished in Hepplewhite, with the sofa and two chairs facing the fireplace.

Anne sat in one of the chairs and ventured a smile. "Did you have something you wished to say to me, my lord?"

He paced about the small space in evident agitation, his brow creased and his hands behind his back held in a tight fist.

He began abruptly. "I saw you with Lord Denzil," he revealed shortly.

"I know. I saw you, and that's why I left with Lord Denzil," she murmured imperturbably, gazing up at him.

"If you intend to make yourself a byword in London by sitting in that devil's pocket, I demand that you leave London at once. I will not have a scandal."

"Well, no one has asked you to have a scandal," she replied.

"Don't be flippant with me, my girl. I'm exercising the greatest restraint at this moment to not take you over my knee and deliver of you a good spanking."

Anne smiled, her teeth clenched. "I'm so glad you're exercising restraint. It's so mature of you."

He gave her a withering look.

"And will you stop pacing about in that manner?" she demanded pettishly. "I'm getting a neck ache trying to follow you."

"I've had a neck ache since the first day I saw you."

"How gallant of you to say so," she sniffed.

He waved an impatient hand. "Let's stop the fara-diddles. Either you desist from hanging on Denzil's sleeve or you leave London immediately."

It was an ultimatum delivered with perfect serious-ness. It gave Anne the greatest pleasure to remind him, "I think you've forgotten about my diary, my lord."

He gave her a long look. "I think you'd best forget your diary."

"Oh, but I couldn't! It has so many memories be-tween its covers."

"All about you and Simon and God knows how many other men between the covers, right, my lady?" he said harshly.

She almost jumped at his tone, but smiled and said demurely, folding her hands on her lap, "That and other things."

He stopped and towered over her. "One would think you'd have too much decency to inflict such filth upon the world!"

Her temper flared at this, and she flung herself up out of her chair, pushing him away. "According to you, I have no decency at all, my lord. So why should considerations of decency hold any weight with me?" She began to pace about the room in the highest dud-geon.

He followed her perambulations with a narrowed gaze. After a moment, he said, "I wish you'd burn that damned diary."

"No doubt you do," she said cordially. "But I won't, so you may put that idea out of your head. I won't burn my diary, and I won't leave London until I please."

"I hope you're careful with that thing. It could be stolen, you know."

She stopped and turned slowly toward him, an arrested gaze on her face. So it could. She tilted her head and smiled at him. "Oh, I'm most careful with it, my lord. I keep it under my pillow at night."

His lips curled. "And during the day?"

"About," she said vaguely, casting a demure but significant glance downward.

His eyes widened as though he were struck with a most horrible suspicion, and he swept his gaze searchingly over her person. She was dressed fashionably in a skintight muslin gown that had been dampened to cling to her figure. His gaze became very intent indeed.

Anne cleared her throat after enduring a few moments of his roving gaze and eyed him roguishly. He blushed to the roots of his hair.

"Was there anything else you wished, my lord?" she asked innocently.

He ground his teeth. "I could wish you to the devil, but I'm too much of a gentleman to say so," he spat out.

He had managed to make his sentiments felt anyway, gentleman or no. "Fancy Denzil's devilish enough for me." She smiled smugly.

He took two steps toward her and grasped her shoulders. "You're not to see Denzil anymore," he said furiously. "He's a scoundrel, and I won't have you associating with him."

She shook out of his grasp, her breathing quickened. "He's a scoundrel, and I'm a wicked widow. I am going to associate with him, and there's nothing you can do to stop me. As a matter of fact—" her face took on a determined set "—I've already promised to accompany Denzil to the Pantheon Masquerade tomorrow night." Her eyes glittered dangerously.

His mouth dropped. "The Pantheon Masquerade? Are you lost to all sense of propriety? Of all the places in the world to go…" He sputtered, then stopped, too angry to speak further.

She stepped quickly to the door. "I know you don't think the Pantheon Masquerade at all the thing, Pastor Max, but I'm quite looking forward to it. I hear there's a great deal of license encouraged in the behavior of those wearing disguises. Who could ask for more?"

And with that, she turned and fled from the room.

She ascended the stairs at a rapid pace and burst into her room, her face red with anger. Pastor Max was the most heavy-handed tyrant. She would show him. She deliberately took a piece of hot-pressed paper from her little secrétaire and sat down, picking up a quill pen. Dipping it in ink, she composed a hasty message, then sealed it with a wafer. She rang the bell for her abigail and tapped her fingers impatiently until Lucy entered the room at a scurry.

"Here, Lucy, I want you to take this letter and have a runner deliver it immediately to Lord Denzil. I think his house is in Berkeley Square. The runner should wait for a reply."

The girl stood stock-still in apparent shock at this request. Anne laughed at her expression. "You needn't be in a worry. There's nothing clandestine about it." She knew that if she had called for Tilly, she wouldn't have got away with this statement so easily.

Lucy, suppressing a sigh of relief, hastened to assure her mistress that such a thought had never entered her head; then she curtsied and ran from the room.

Anne pulled open her armoire and rummaged through the piles of clothes and bandboxes on the shelves. After a short search, she took down a box from the top shelf and laid it on the bed.

She pulled off the lid, parting the silver tissue paper, and revealed a very lovely, exquisitely made pink silk domino. Anne held the cloak up to her and smiled. It would look most becomingly, she had no doubt. She bent and retrieved from the floor a rose-pink half-mask that was an accessory to the domino. Not go to the Pantheon Masquerade? Max had to be all about in his head.

Denzil's letter, brought in by a puffing Lucy, was florid indeed with expressions of gratitude for her changed sentiments. He would look for her most expressly at the Pantheon.

AT SUPPER Anne informed Lady Byrne of her plans for the next evening. The duchess looked at Anne blankly for a moment. "But I thought we were going to the play at Covent Garden. Are you certain you wish to go? I don't like masquerades myself. Neither does Max, actually. He's much too fastidious for them. I don't like them because of the nuisance-mask you have to wear. Somehow or other it always covers my eyes, and I bump about blindly for the rest of the evening. It's most vexatious, I needn't tell you."

Anne soon prevailed upon her, however, expressing her desire to go to the masquerade most persuasively. She had never been to a masquerade. She'd heard they were most diverting. Wouldn't Lady Byrne please, please be so kind as to give her this high treat?

Lady Byrne laughed, shaking her head. "You certainly know how to cut a wheedle, my dear. Well, if you're so set upon it, we shall go. But, I daresay you won't like it above half."

So the next evening, after a small party at the Mendleshams', the Byrne carriage was directed toward the Pantheon, situated on the south side of Oxford Street. It was a most magnificent structure, decorated in a florid style. It comprised a large suite of salons and a ballroom, which was a huge rectangular hall with a painted ceiling, a raised platform for the musicians and numerous boxes and discreet alcoves. Crystal chandeliers hung from the ceiling and from every Gothic arch that lined the room. Originally it had been patronized only by members of the haut ton, but the company soon deteriorated so greatly that the Marquess of Crewe had every excuse for not wishing Anne to attend there.

The ballroom was filled to overflowing with merrymakers intriguingly garbed in dominoes and historical costumes. Pierrots and Columbines danced about. A parti-colored Harlequin swept across the floor. There were Hamlets and Elizabeths and a most lascivious Cleopatra who caused Lady Byrne to close her eyes in embarrassment and give a shuddering cry of protest. It was very noisy, very gay and very dangerous, for all were behaving with the license encouraged by the wearing of masks. Anne was jostled about as she stood next to a decorated pillar, and, to her horror, was actually pinched by a complete stranger!

She had an impulse to grab Lady Byrne's nerveless hand and flee from the place. But she quelled it, spying Lord Denzil in a spangled purple domino bearing down upon her. His mask was spangled and trimmed with lace, and he sported spangled high heels as well. Only Lord Denzil could be wearing such a get-up as that.

"Ah, Lady Severne," he exclaimed, taking Anne's hand and giving it a lingering kiss, executing a most profound bow. "I could not mistake you. You look as beautiful as a rose."

Anne snatched back her hand and smiled tremulously at him. Lady Byrne gave a disgusted snort. He turned to the ballroom floor and made a gesture with his purple-gloved hand. "Would you do me the honor?"

A quadrille was being set in motion, and Anne steeled herself to take his proffered arm and accompany him to the floor. The crowded dance floor was hot and stuffy and the music could barely be heard, but these discomforts were as naught compared to the discomfort caused by Lord Denzil's outrageous flirtations with her.

It was soon borne in upon Anne that Denzil assumed her to be eager to accept these advances and that the Pantheon Masquerade was the perfect place to display them. He chucked her chin and tried to put his hand about her waist in a manner that she most disliked. He was extremely difficult to repulse. And to make matters worse, his breath reeked of spirits and he showed a tendency to sway on his feet. Quite repugnant.

It was with unalloyed and heartfelt rejoicing that Anne noted the entrance of the Marquess of Crewe accompanied by Ninian and Geoffrey Stanhope. He had come to drag her, by force, out of this den of iniquity, no doubt. Once again, she thought, prudishness had its points. He was wearing a most sober domino of pure black and a serviceable half-mask. Its hue suited his nature, but Anne felt she would have recognized his tall, straight form had he been wearing flaming scarlet.

She turned away quickly, not wishing to be espied by him. She had a little charade she wished to play. Out of the corner of her eye, she saw him separate from Ninian and Stanhope to speak with his aunt, who was sitting in a chair by the wall.

When the set was finished, she excused herself and flew toward Ninian and Stanhope, pulling them into an alcove.

Mr. Stanhope blushed rosily and put up a stammering and inarticulate protest at this cavalier treatment, and Ninian disdainfully removed Anne's hand from his golden sleeve, saying, "Really, my dear bit o'muslin, times must be getting pretty rough when you have to waylay customers."

Anne gasped and burst out laughing. When she could speak, she said in a reproachful tone, "For shame, gentlemen, for shame, to accuse me of being so wanton a creature. I shall never be able to look you in the eye again."

Realizing their mistake, they both fell over themselves to apologize. Anne, after a few moments of pouting, relented, giving a little chuckle. "What would Miss Farlow think of you, Mr. Stanhope," she teased, "if she learned you associated with bits o' muslin?"

The more you love romance ... the more you'll love this offer

FREE!

*Mail this heart today!
(See inside)*

**Join us on a Harlequin Honeymoon
and we'll give you
4 free books
A free makeup mirror and brush kit
And a free mystery gift**

IT'S A
HARLEQUIN HONEYMOON—
A SWEETHEART
OF A FREE OFFER!
HERE'S WHAT YOU GET:

1. **Four New Harlequin Presents Novels—FREE!**
   Take a Harlequin Honeymoon with your four exciting romances—yours FREE from Harlequin Reader Service. Each of these hot-off-the-press novels brings you the passion and tenderness of today's greatest love stories…your free passports to bright new worlds of love and foreign adventure.

2. **A Lighted Makeup Mirror and Brush Kit—FREE!**
   This lighted makeup mirror and brush kit allows plenty of light for those quick touch-ups. It operates on two easy-to-replace batteries and bulbs (batteries not included). It holds everything you need for a perfect finished look yet is small enough to slip into your purse or pocket—4-⅛" x 3" closed.

3. **An Exciting Mystery Bonus—FREE!**
   You'll be thrilled with this surprise gift. It is a useful and attractive item and will be the source of many compliments.

4. **Money-Saving Home Delivery!**
   Join Harlequin Reader Service and enjoy the convenience of previewing eight new books every month delivered right to your home. Each book is yours for only $1.95—30¢ less per book than what you pay in stores—plus 89¢ postage and handling per shipment. Great savings plus total convenience add up to a sweetheart of a deal for you!

5. **Free Newsletter**
   It's *heart to heart*, the indispensable insider's look at our most popular writers, upcoming books, even recipes from your favorite authors.

6. **More Surprise Gifts**
   Because our home subscribers are our most valued readers, we'll be sending you additional free gifts from time to time—as a token of our appreciation.

START YOUR HARLEQUIN HONEYMOON TODAY—JUST
COMPLETE, DETACH AND MAIL YOUR FREE-OFFER CARD

Get your fabulous gifts
ABSOLUTELY FREE!

MAIL THIS CARD TODAY.

PLACE
HEART STICKER
HERE

GIVE YOUR HEART TO HARLEQUIN

YES! Please send me my four Harlequin Presents novels FREE, along with my free lighted makeup mirror and brush kit and free mystery gift as explained on the opposite page.

NAME _____
(PLEASE PRINT)

ADDRESS _____ APT. ____

CITY _____ PROV. ____

POSTAL CODE _____

308 CIP U1BS

PRICES SUBJECT TO CHANGE. OFFER LIMITED TO ONE PER HOUSEHOLD AND NOT VALID TO PRESENT SUBSCRIBERS.

HARLEQUIN READER SERVICE "NO RISK" GUARANTEE

— There's no obligation to buy—and the free books and gifts remain yours to keep.
— You pay the lowest price possible and receive books before they appear in stores.
— You may end your subscription anytime—just write and let us know.

PRINTED IN U.S.A.

START YOUR
HARLEQUIN HONEYMOON TODAY.
JUST COMPLETE, DETACH AND MAIL YOUR
FREE OFFER CARD.

If offer card below is missing, write to: Harlequin Reader Service, P.O. Box 609
Fort Erie, Ontario L2A 5X3

DETACH AND MAIL TODAY!

**Business
Reply Mail**

No Postage Stamp
Necessary if Mailed
in Canada

Postage will be paid by

Harlequin Reader Service®

P.O. Box 609
Fort Erie, Ontario
L2A 9Z9

Canada Post
Postes Canada
125

At the mention of Miss Farlow, Mr. Stanhope was rendered idiotically ecstatic. He could only sigh and give a soulful face.

Ninian rolled his eyes. "Don't know why you mentioned her name, Lady Anne. He'll act like a love-struck mooncalf for the rest of the night."

"I hope not." Anne smiled. "Because I am greatly in need of his services. And yours."

"I am willing to do anything you ask of me," Ninian said promptly, giving a leg. Stanhope nodded his willingness, too.

"Dispose of Denzil for me, will you? He's plaguing me to death, and there's something I wish to do."

Ninian's eyes goggled and he stared at her, a good deal shocked. He swallowed and swung his eyes surreptitiously back and forth. "I'll do anything for you, my lady, but I must cut my stick at murder," he informed her in a hushed voice.

She was taken aback. "Murder?" she exclaimed. Then she choked and gave a laugh. "Really, what a Ninian you are!" She shook her head at him. "I only want you to get Denzil to leave this building—immediately."

"Oh!" He wiped his brow. "What a relief." Then his eyes danced, and he fastened his hand on Stanhope's sleeve. "Come on, man. We must be doing."

Anne, hidden in the alcove, watched them as they stalked their prey. They elbowed resolutely through the crowd and then circled around the unwary Denzil. Anne wondered what they had in mind. She could have blessed them for their expeditiousness. For, quite simply, Stanhope gave Denzil a mighty push while Ninian planted his foot on Denzil's cape. The domino ripped at the seams. And Denzil actually screamed with horror. He berated Ninian and Stanhope quite loudly as clodpoles and blocks, but they hustled him out of the room, under the pretext that he was indecently exposed in a public place.

Anne sighed with pleasure and then cast her eyes about in search of her prey. Crewe had left Lady Byrne. He was searching the floor with his gaze, obviously trying to find Anne in order to pounce upon her and force her to leave.

She gave a wicked smile and then crept slowly toward him, maneuvering so that his back was to her and he was unable to see her approach. When she reached him, she looked around to make certain Lady Byrne wasn't watching, and then she put her hands on his broad shoulders and stretched on tiptoe.

"No, don't turn, Lord Denzil," she whispered. "I don't want Lady Byrne to see us talking." She blew in his ear and tickled it with a light finger. Crewe stiffened, becoming positively rigid. She bit down a laugh and then said in a caressing voice, "My bedroom is on the second floor in the back of the house. There's a convenient tree. I always keep the window open. And—" she turned his head with a slight pressure of her hands and kissed him full on the lips "—I sleep very lightly." And with that, she released him and sped away.

CHAPTER SEVEN

Anne sat in the carriage next to Lady Byrne on the way home, biting her lips and exercising the greatest restraint not to fall into the whoops. She had been outrageous, she knew. But, oh, how deliciously funny! How she wished Pastor Max hadn't been wearing a mask so she could have seen the expression on his face when she delivered into his astonished ear her lover-like message. Just thinking of it almost overset her.

He must have been shocked, no doubt. But she did not feel even a twinge of compunction. According to him, her character was already beneath contempt, so what need she care if he continued to think badly of her? The pompous lobcock. It would serve him right if he did sustain a severe shock.

She hoped that she had so thoroughly discomposed him that he would be betrayed into uncharacteristic behavior. She considered what his subsequent actions might be and hoped they might include the calling of Denzil out for a duel. That would kill two birds with one stone. But she conjectured that his anger would be directed more at herself than at Denzil, so whatever he did in reaction to her Pantheon ploy, she would probably bear the brunt of it.

She would be happy to bear the brunt of whatever Crewe did, so long as it was perfectly scandalous. He had certainly proved a difficult fox to run to ground.

He was almost like an impregnable citadel that she was laying siege to. A prince in his own white tower. Well, she itched to pull him down from his divine height, and she thought she was perhaps on the right path at last for succeeding to do so.

The carriage arrived at Byrne House, and Anne and the duchess quickly alighted, Lady Byrne expressing a desire to take to her bed immediately. The Pantheon Masquerade had not been at all to her liking.

"I can't abide going to parties where I don't know anyone who's there," she explained, suppressing a yawn. "And a masquerade is even worse, because people that you know may indeed be there, but you can't tell that they are because they're in disguise!"

Anne nodded sympathetically. "How perfectly true. It is most aggravating." She lifted her skirts as they ascended the stairs and asked, indifferently, "Did you recognize anyone there?"

Lady Byrne creased her brow. "No, I don't think so. Max was there, but I didn't precisely recognize him because he marched right up to me and announced himself. And if he hadn't done so, I don't think I would ever have believed it was Max. I was never more surprised."

"Why?" Anne asked as they reached the landing.

Lady Byrne opened her blue eyes wide. "Well, but I told you. Max never attends masquerades! My mouth actually dropped when he announced himself."

"Did he say why he was there?"

"No. He simply asked where you were, and I said you were about. I daresay he went to keep his eye on us to ensure that nothing untoward occurred to upset us."

"Such as being pinched by a complete stranger?" Anne grumbled, rubbing the afflicted spot.

Lady Byrne gasped. "No! Were you pinched?"

Anne nodded.

Lady Byrne's hands covered her cheeks in undisguised horror. "How terrible for you!" she exclaimed. "You must take to your bed at once. You must be feeling positively faint. No wonder you were so silent on the way home. I'll send in Mrs. Fardle to bring you some laudanum drops. I wish I had my smelling salts with me. How vexatious. Do you want some burnt pastilles?" She looked at Anne anxiously.

Anne couldn't speak for a moment. Then with just a quiver in her voice, she said, "You must think me very depraved, for I have no intention of succumbing to a fit of the vapors because I was pinched. It was unnerving, but I survived."

Lady Byrne tilted her head uncertainly. "I don't think you depraved, my dear. Only very, very brave. Most admirable." She sighed and closed her eyes. "You are inspiring. But don't overdo it, my dear. You'll have a reaction in the morning." She opened her eyes, a grave expression on her face. "One thing is certain. We shall never go to the Pantheon again!" After this terrible decree, she gave Anne a warm embrace, patting her tenderly on the back. "You must go to bed, and at once."

Anne, choking with laughter, was only too ready to comply with her aunt's directions and nearly flew to her room. Her abigail helped her out of her domino and pulled back the bedclothes. Anne dismissed her and climbed into bed, still thinking of Max.

THE NEXT MORNING, Lord Crewe came to invite Anne for a ride to Richmond Park. Anne had to decline, for she had an engagement in the afternoon and knew it would take most of the day to ride out to Richmond Park and back.

"It was most kind of you to ask me, my lord," she said, watching him with a lurking smile in her eyes. "I hear the flowers are very pretty."

"They are indeed. It is a setting most worthy of you. I shall be happy to show you it another time." He bowed slightly, and Anne assimilated his words with a gasp.

"Flattery from my lord Crewe," she observed with widened eyes. "How unusual."

He stared at her coolly. "I've no doubt you're very used to flattery from your many lo—suitors."

Her eyebrows raised at this near slip. Her lips pursed. "Very true, my lord. And I'm completely inured to it."

"Not from Lord Denzil's lips," he shot out.

She looked him up and down. He was holding himself most stiffly. More so than usual, as a matter of fact. His face, too, was stiff. Only his eyes betrayed the slightest bit of emotion. And they were actually burning at her. She felt her blood kindle with excitement, and she quickly picked up this gage.

"Ah, but Lord Denzil's lips are so fascinating. Anything that comes from them must be acceptable."

"Even kisses?" His bantering tone was underlined with harshness.

She looked down demurely, a slight smile curving her lips as an answer.

His fists clenched. "You will not see Lord Denzil again," he commanded.

"I won't?"

"No, you won't," he said, less certainly. "You disobeyed my wishes by going to the masquerade last night, but you won't disobey me again."

"How do you know I was at the masquerade last night?" she asked, looking up quickly. "Were you there?"

He didn't answer for a moment. "What matters if I were? Lady Byrne told me you went and were met by Lord Denzil."

Anne wanted to crow with triumph. He was being evasive. The Pastor Max was not quite so forthright as usual. She bowed her head, hiding a smile, and accepted this information with indifference, not defending her actions in the least.

He looked most put out by her demure front, but she halted further remonstrances with a gesture. "I hope you'll excuse me, my lord," she said, rising lightly from her chair. "It is always so diverting to speak with you. But I have a number of errands to execute this morning and must prepare for an expedition down Bond Street."

"Are you going alone?"

She frowned at this sudden question. "Why, no. I shall be attended by a maid."

"I shall drive you."

It was not a request, and she bridled at his autocratic tone. "Really, my lord, I have no desire to put you out. I shall be most happy to go with my maid."

"I'm sure you would," he said grimly. "But I shall go with you."

She stared at him in consternation; then comprehension stole into her eyes. "What, you think I've made an assignation to meet with someone clandestinely?'' she asked in patent disbelief.

"I wouldn't put it past you," he muttered, and she immediately turned and flounced from the room to run up the stairs for her chip straw hat and pink gloves. She informed Lady Byrne, who was reclining on a sofa in her bedroom, that Lord Crewe had kindly offered his services for the morning and was going to drive her to Bond Street.

"How very good of him," her aunt exclaimed, her face lighting up with pleasure. "Max is so considerate. Suggest that he stop in when you return." Anne nodded and prepared to leave the room but was stopped. "Oh, yes, and Anne, don't forget to purchase that chicken-skin fan we saw at the shop the other day. And a stick of my favorite perfume."

"I won't forget." She turned to sail down the stairs to the waiting marquess. He was tapping his foot impatiently, and she smiled at him brightly as she stepped out the door.

His groom was leading his grays up and down the street and pulled up at the sight of his master. Crewe helped Anne into the curricle, then climbed up himself, taking hold of the reins while the groom stood up behind.

"Where to, my lady?" Max inquired coldly.

"I have quite a number of places to visit," she said, a trifle maliciously. She hoped she was ruining his morning. "But first on the list is Hookham's Library."

He set the horses in motion with a flick of the whip. His mouth curled in distaste. "Not to buy a new romance novel, I hope."

Her eyes danced. "Why not? I think they make very edifying reading."

He turned his head to look at her, his eyes hard. "One would suppose your diary would provide sufficient edification for reading."

"You might find it so," she said, almost to herself, thinking that what he expected and what he would find written in her diary would provide him with a most enlightening experience.

"Would you let me read it?"

It was her turn to look at him, her eyes wide. His profile looked most determined, and she nodded in quick understanding. "Do you take me for a flat? If you had it in your hands, my lord, you'd burn it," she accused him.

"Without hesitation. I would then have you leave London so fast it would make your head spin."

As he looked absolutely enamored of such a prospect, she couldn't help but frown at him. She turned a pointed shoulder and noticed that they had entered the busy Bond Street. A number of curricles and carriages crowded the way, and on the pavement, fashionables were strolling about. Toasts in striped spencers with matching parasols, Pinks in pale pantaloons and shining Hessians and Bond Street Beaux with their nipped-in coats and quizzing glasses were all on the strut. She watched them with wide-eyed interest, such a picture they presented, until her attention was recalled by Lord Crewe's dry voice.

"Are you looking for anyone?" he asked tersely.

She shrugged airily. "For whom would I be looking?"

"Lord Denzil, perhaps?" he growled.

"Quite possibly."

His mouth tightened, and he was quiet for a moment. "I see you are determined to add to the adventures already chronicled in your diary," he said, with an attempt at a light tone. Most assiduously, he studied his hands holding the reins. "But, the conquest of Lord Denzil could not offer very interesting reading, he being already a confirmed rake. Why don't you take up an offer from me instead?"

Her hand clutched at the side of the carriage. She closed her mouth and swallowed with difficulty. "What offer?" she asked in a hoarse voice.

"An invitation to dine at my house tonight," he disclosed in a hurried tone. His color was heightened, and Anne's head jerked forward as she stared at him in the deepest suspicion.

"Alone?" she whispered.

"Yes, alone," he repeated with a touch of asperity.

"For what reason?" she asked with narrowed eyes.

"To become better acquainted with you, of course."

His eyes hadn't left his hands yet. Anne tapped her fingers. Too smoky by half. He had presented his most unprecedented invitation with an air of calmness that was just too suspicious. Something was afoot. She forced her voice to sound mocking. "I can hardly credit my hearing. What an immodest proposal, Pastor Max. Eat at your house alone?"

He thrust out his strong chin. "We are relatives."

"Only through marriage," she pointed out.

"Makes no odds."

"Well—" her throat tightened with excitement "—if it makes no odds to you, it can certainly make no odds to me. I accept your gracious invitation."

"I shall send my carriage for you at eight."

Her eyes widened with incredulity and her mouth twisted with a crooked smile as she said, "Most obliging of you."

He did not reply, since the bow windows of the Hookham Library came into view at this moment. He pulled his horses up before this establishment. "I'll wait for you," he informed her, and Anne nodded absently, her mind seething with conjecture as the groom helped her down from the curricle.

THAT EVENING Anne watched Lady Byrne's departure in her coach for Lady Cork's house with ill-contained excitement. She had with difficulty convinced Lady Byrne to attend Lady Cork's without her, crying a headache. She did not mention her real plans for the evening. Lady Byrne would no doubt have said an invitation to Lady Cork's held precedence over dinner with Max. She would also have exclaimed at his unusual behavior, demanding he cancel his engagement with Anne and come to dinner at Byrne House instead. But Anne had absolutely no desire to have her engagement with Crewe canceled. Dinner alone with him. How incredible. She couldn't understand why the prospect excited her so. And the casual manner in which he had delivered his invitation, without any explanations at all, was also incredible. There had to be a reason for his about-face, his compliments. Max had some ill-intentioned purpose, she had no doubt, but she could not tell what it might be. It was not common practice for a lady of quality to dine alone with a gentleman at his home. It was no less than an invitation to be raped. She did not, however, think that Max had designs on her virtue. She was looking forward to this dinner party.

She arrayed herself most becomingly in a gown of yellow brocade with her golden hair arranged in a riot of ringlets, in the Sappho style. She was wearing no jewelry, and since her gown was low-cut, she was exposing quite an expanse of milk-white skin to any, unspecified, beholder. Not without effect, she hoped.

She took her pair of yellow gloves from Lucy and stared at the girl for a moment with narrowed eyes. If Max had something up his sleeve, it would be best to be prepared. "Lucy," she said suddenly.

"Yes, my lady?"

"Will you do me a favor this evening?"

The girl bobbed a curtsy, her round, pleasant face alert. "Why, anything at all, my lady. What is it?"

Anne wondered a moment how to phrase her request. She frowned as she pulled on her gloves. "I have been sleeping badly these nights," she began.

Lucy exclaimed her solicitude.

"Yes, well, I would be most grateful if you would keep an ear out for me. If I should cry out or anything during the night, would you please run right in here, without knocking, to administer me some laudanum drops to help me sleep?"

If Lucy considered this a rather capricious request from her mistress, she was far too well trained to say so aloud. "Of course, my lady," she assured Anne with becoming alacrity. "I shall come in as fast as a pig's whisper at the first peep from you."

Anne was satisfied and descended the stairs to await Lord Crewe's coach. She did not have to wait long.

Reeth, his face creased with bewilderment, entered the drawing room to inform her that Crewe's coach was awaiting her. As he no doubt expected her to be prostrate in bed with a headache, Anne felt it incumbent upon her to come up with some stammered explanation. "I forgot that he was coming to escort me to Lady Cork's until after Lady Byrne had left. It would be too rude to send his carriage away now."

Reeth accepted this information with a wooden countenance, and she could only be grateful for his impassivity, since she knew her excuse was lame indeed. She shrugged, though, hurried out of the room without giving Reeth another glance and sailed down the front steps to be helped into the awaiting carriage. No disapproving stare from a butler would deter her from this night's possibilities.

The Marquess of Crewe's home was situated in Albemarle Street. As the carriage slowed before it, she noted that it was a commanding edifice of many stories, with a stucco front and an imposing portico.

Upon dismounting from the carriage, she was immediately taken into hand by a liveried butler who led her across a vast hall to a mahogany door, which opened into a salon. Anne looked about this room with interest. It was hung with delicate blue paper and had tall windows giving onto the darkened street. There were two couches with gilded scroll ends and crimson upholstery, a satinwood sofa table and some Sheraton chairs. Anne did not scrutinize the furnishings, for the Marquess of Crewe was standing in front of the fireplace, his arm flung casually across the mantel. She did scrutinize him, however, and found him looking complete to a shade in a very elegant evening rig of a blue coat with black pantaloons. For some reason, at the sight of him, her heart started beating rapidly, and she stood still, unable to say a word.

The marquess stepped forward, taking her hand and bending down to kiss it. Her hand shook in his, and she felt as though she had received a shock.

"How happy I am that you have honored me with your presence, my lady," he murmured, his eyes glinting mockingly into hers.

She snatched her hand from his grasp and walked toward the fireplace. "I think the honor is all mine, my lord," she said coolly.

His eyes raked her body. "There would be many who might disagree with that."

She eyed him frowningly, but since his face had a singularly innocent expression on it, she chose not to challenge that statement.

"Would you care for a glass of ratafia, my dear?" he inquired politely.

"What are you drinking?" She indicated the glass in his hand.

"Champagne."

"I shall have some, too. I wish to do justice to this occasion."

He bowed graciously, walked to a sideboard and smoothly poured her a glass. He handed it to her, saying, "Are you certain you would not wish for a milder beverage?"

"Of course not," she denied, surprised at his question.

"I would not care to have a dinner companion who is deep in her cups, you know," he murmured, his eyes hooded and his mouth straight.

"I have a very good head," she declared.

He smiled enigmatically. "That remains to be seen."

"What do you mean by that?" she asked, puzzled.

"Did I mean anything? I wonder." He gave her a dazzling smile, and she suddenly found it difficult to breathe. "Will you be seated, Lady Anne?"

"With pleasure." She seated herself on the sofa trembling, wondering what was the matter with her.

He disposed himself on a Sheraton chair opposite her, a whimsical smile on his face. "Does this not remind you of the first day I made your acquaintance?" he asked conversationally.

"I would prefer not to think of that day."

"Why?"

"It was most unpleasant, and you know it." She tilted her glass and downed the champagne.

"How very strange. Was the learning of your inheritance so unpleasant for you?" he inquired in an interested tone.

Anne bit her lip. The inheritance. Lord, she had clean forgotten it. "In a way, my lord, it was." She wet her lips. "Simon should have had the enjoyment of that fortune during his life."

His face became black. "If it had not been for you, my dear Lady Anne, he would have done so," he growled, his hand reaching out to grip her wrist tightly.

"If your father had not been so damned tyrannical, my dear Pastor Max, he would have done so."

They glared at each other.

Sutton, Crewe's butler, presented a most timely interruption at that moment by entering the room to announce dinner. Crewe had to muster all his civility to release Anne's wrist and then proffer his arm, and she had to muster all hers to take it.

"The menu has been most carefully selected," Crewe informed Anne as they seated themselves opposite each other at the ends of a long mahogany table. "I hope you will enjoy it."

"I'm sure I will," she murmured. The table, she noticed, was covered with a snowy cloth, and the many candles placed upon it made the Spode dinner setting sparkle with light. There was a silver epergne in the middle; vases of yellow roses were set out at intervals.

Dinner consisted of three courses, the first two served by footmen who remained in attendance as Anne and Lord Crewe exchanged polite inanities. Braised turbot in champagne was accompanied by duck paté and crab Parisienne with a white wine sauce. Anne partook of large portions of the braised turbot, much to Lord Crewe's evident approval.

The covers were removed, and veal à la crème with a side of French beans, all simmered in wine, lamb cutlets in pastry with wine gravy and chicken with wine sauce were placed before them. Despite being watched closely by Lord Crewe, Anne was enjoying both a second glass of champagne and the meal itself. She had never tasted such delicious food. She commented as much, and Crewe gave a slight nod.

"My chef will be most gratified," he murmured.

His tone was slightly supercilious, and Anne lapsed again into silence, engrossed with her veal à la crème.

Lord Crewe did not initiate any conversation, and all of Anne's polite essays were met with indifference and a touch of boredom. She reached for her champagne and took a deep draft. The marquess was certainly not an ideal host. In fact, he was a boor. Why had he invited her if he wasn't even going to talk to her? She should have known it would be like this. She was so angry by the time the second course was removed that she felt hot and dizzy. The room seemed to swim about her, and she closed her eyes for a moment. It must have been a long moment, for by the time she reopened them, the third course had been deftly served and, to Anne's astonishment, all the footmen had been dismissed. She was alone with Lord Crewe.

She assimilated this fact with mixed feelings as she took a small spoonful of the champagne sorbet, having refused the iced chestnut soufflé in sherry and the baked apples in brandy. She took several spoonfuls of the sorbet before she mustered enough courage to ask, with insouciance, "My Lord Crewe, is this the first time you've entertained a woman alone in your home?" She gave him a coy glance from under her eyelashes and tipped her lips into an engaging smile.

He seemed unmoved by her tactics. "If I said no, you would revile me for my rakish ways, and if I said yes, you would stigmatize me as a priggish boor. I believe I shall say nothing at all."

"That was quite a mouthful for saying nothing," she observed sapiently. "You are most careful, are you not? You needn't be. *I* don't judge people!" She said this with sufficient force to make his brows lift.

"Meaning I do?"

Her answer was written on her face, and he looked at her thoughtfully.

She tried to read his expression, but for some reason, it was blurred. She blinked once or twice, wishing she could move the candles away. Their glare was giving her a headache.

"I daresay this is not the first time you've been entertained by a gentleman alone," he said suddenly.

"Besides Simon." He frowned. "Perhaps I shouldn't say gentlemen. Just other men."

"Other men?" she repeated blankly, his words just barely sinking in as she took a lingering spoonful of her champagne sorbet. "What other men?"

He sneered unpleasantly. "What a perfect little innocent you are, Lady Anne. What other men? That's rich."

She pushed her dish away and eyed him with undisguised hostility. "You are intolerable. I daresay it must be enviable to be so pure and unsullied in character that you can place yourself on some Olympian height from which you can look down upon everyone else." She swallowed convulsively after this difficult speech.

"I don't place myself on too high a form, Lady Anne," he said disdainfully. "Nor do I place myself on too low a form, either."

"Meaning I do?"

The answer was to be read on his face.

She took a deep breath. "If we don't change the subject, my lord, I think we shall soon be at daggers' drawing."

He certainly seemed ready to accommodate her. Without a visible effort, he said, quite conversationally, "Which country out of all the countries you've graced with your presence did you prefer? Austria? Germany? France?"

Her eyes narrowed. Now she knew why he had invited her to dinner. To talk her into leaving London. Well, he would fail. "Obviously, you're hoping I shall remove myself to one of them without delay. Well, I'm sorry to have to disappoint you, my lord. I'm in my favorite country at this very moment."

He snorted. "England? Don't expect me to believe that." He looked at her with what she thought was a sneer. "You didn't spend a month of your marriage here."

She turned her head away and looked down. Her head felt oddly heavy. With difficulty, she murmured, "Not through my choice."

"Through Simon's?"

His response had been rapier-quick. Too quick for her. Without thinking and with her head still bent, she said, "Of course. He hated England. Hated his home, his family. Everything. He liked living on the Continent, going from gaming house to gaming house, living the life of a—" She broke off, confused. What was she saying? She passed her hand over her head. Everything seemed to be vaporish. In a peeved voice, she asked, "Is the fire giving off smoke, my lord?"

"No."

"Oh." She took a deep breath and forced herself to raise her head and meet his eyes. He was watching her.

"Is the room too warm for you?" he asked after a pause.

She was feeling very hot, but she shook her head most politely.

"Are you feeling well?" He studied her keenly. Her face was probably flushed, and he confirmed her suspicions when he said, "Don't tell me you're suffering from any discomfort at being alone with a man."

"Of course not."

A strange expression came into his eyes. Almost burning. "I wonder if you miss being with a man." She glared at him, and he smoothly amended his speech. "With Simon, I mean."

"God, no!" She said this with such vehemence that he smiled a mirthless smile and said, "One would almost assume you were glad to be rid of him. It must bring you great satisfaction to know that his death was all through your own doing."

"It wasn't!" she flashed.

His eyebrow lifted. "It wasn't a satisfaction?"

"It wasn't my doing. I had nothing to do with it. Simon was drunk. He had fuzzed the cards. He was caught..." Her voice dropped off, and she stared at her plate.

"That is a pretty hard story to swallow."

"You're determined to think badly of me," she said in a stifled voice.

"Your own husband thought badly of you. And with reason."

He was being deliberately cruel. She could feel it. Feeding his own wrath with accusations that he dared her to deny. Something in her snapped, and she raised her head to stare at him with flashing eyes. "You didn't know Simon. How can you believe anything he said?" She couldn't see him—her eyes were too blinded with tears—and she was shaking. "I didn't even know him. Until it was too late. He was weak and mean and selfish. How could you not know your own brother?" Then she covered her mouth. His own brother. How awful of her to hurt him with this knowledge. Let him think of her what he would. It was wrong for her to destroy his memory of his brother. She gave a strange laugh. "You don't believe me, of course. How wise. I'm not myself. I don't know what came over me." She stood up uncertainly. "I would like to go home." She took one step and the room spun. The floor seemed to leap up at her, and she swayed but was caught up suddenly and held so tightly she couldn't breathe. She put her hand against something that felt as hard as a rock. It was Crewe's chest. She looked up uncertainly to find his eyes glittering into hers.

She tried to speak. Tried to protest. Her mouth opened, quivering, and Crewe bent his gaze to stare at it. Suddenly, his mouth swooped down on hers in a suffocating kiss.

She felt a sharp thrill shoot through her as his arms tightened around her in a close embrace. She started to push him away but somehow couldn't. She felt molded to him, and she became dizzy with the sensations that coursed through her.

He lifted his head, and Anne let out a choked sob. His face was intense with passion, and he stared down at her a breathless moment. She could only stare back, standing weakly in his arms, bewildered.

"You are a witch!" he hissed, and with irresistible force, he pushed her away. She stumbled against the table but retained her balance by putting her hand on it.

His words cleared the mist that threatened to overcome her. "*I'm* a witch!" she exclaimed, fury boiling through her. "You take advantage of me, and then call me a witch. Well, what you are, my lord, is—"

"Don't say it," his voice ripped. "You'll regret it in the morning." He looked grim. "As I shall regret this."

"I'm regretting this now. You should be ashamed of yourself. How dare you kiss me like that?"

His hands shot out and gripped her arms. "Outraged virtue sounds odd coming from you." She tried to struggle out of his grasp, but his hands only tightened, and he pulled her close to him so their faces almost touched. "You wanted me to kiss you!"

"I did not!" she exclaimed, unnerved by the suppressed violence of his tone. "You're horrible, and I never want to see you again!" And with that, to her own astonishment, she burst into tears.

He stared at her blankly. Then his face softened perceptibly, and a gleam came into his eye. He gently released her. Anne stood there, furious with herself for behaving like a damned watering pot. She couldn't imagine what was the matter with her. Crewe took out his pocket handkerchief and gallantly wiped the tears from her eyes. "It seems I have been taking advantage of you, after all," he acknowledged in an amused voice. "For one of your self-acclaimed ability, you haven't much of a head, have you?"

She sniffed audibly. "I beg your pardon?" Her eyelids began to droop.

"No, it is I who should beg your pardon. My dinner menu was more effective than I dared hope."

She shook her head, unable to understand. She yawned and said weakly, "I would like to go home, my lord."

"Of course."

She was led willy-nilly out of the dining room and into the carriage. There must have been a few minutes to wait for the carriage to be readied, but she didn't notice them. And as soon as they seated themselves and the door was shut behind them, Anne leaned her head against the squabs and drifted off to sleep.

She came to consciousness when the carriage jerked to a halt and found she was resting her head against the marquess's strong shoulder. He did not object to her use of him, so she did not venture an apology. She did not feel up to it. Nor did she feel up to protesting when Crewe competently took her in his arms, as though she were a featherweight, and carried her into the house. He did not relinquish her to a footman, and he spurned Reeth's solicitations without explanation. Reeth hovered behind as Crewe started to carry her up to her room.

Anne, who was slowly regaining her mental acuity, roused herself in protest. "Let me down, if you please," she said with great dignity.

Crewe set her down and watched with interest as she attempted to negotiate the stairs. It was impossible, and she found herself clinging helplessly to the banister, a position she felt she would have to stay in until morning. But Crewe rescued her by sweeping her up in his arms again and going up the stairs with great agility, followed by the clucking Reeth.

In her room he deposited her tenderly upon her bed, bade her good night and left, followed by Reeth.

The bed was very soft and comfortable and just what she had been needing all evening. She curled up, still in her evening dress, and readied herself to drift off to sleep. She didn't do so completely, however, because she kept feeling the strength of Crewe's arms around her and his lips against hers. She lay for some time engaged in pleasant reveries. Suddenly a noise jerked her to wide-eyed awareness. She stiffened as her door creaked open. She peered into the darkness. There was the sound of a stealthy step, and she could just make out a groping figure. The figure stepped into a shaft of moonlight from the window, and Crewe's face was cast into sharp relief.

She almost gasped in indignation. He had left with Reeth, but he was back. And alone! In her bedchamber. She started to wonder what the devil he was doing but realized almost immediately that he was up to no good. For, moving very carefully so as not to disturb her, he bent beside her bed and inched his hand under her pillow. He was searching for her diary!

She thought fast. Her first impulse was to fling herself out of bed and revile him for an underhanded sneaksby. Instead, when his hand was completely under her pillow, she simply rolled over on top of it.

"What the devil!" he snapped, exasperated. He was trapped! Anne had to bite her lip to suppress a giggle. She felt like chortling with glee. She had finally placed the Pastor Max in a compromising position!

He knelt down and carefully tried to pull his arm from underneath her. Still pretending to be fast asleep, she pressed her weight down as hard as she could so that, with another curse, he was forced to tug with vigor. She let him tug away for a few moments, and then quickly she lifted her weight and he fell flat on his back, his head knocking on the floor.

A door slammed, and there was the sound of running footsteps. Anne waited expectantly, but Crewe, with great presence of mind, scooted under the bed like a shot. Lucy burst into the room, armed with the glass of laudanum and water.

"Here, my lady," she cried. "Drink this quick! You'll feel better in a trice." She was holding a candelabrum, and as she stepped up to her mistress's bed, she saw that her mistress was lying there fully clothed. "What, here now!" she exclaimed in surprise. "You still dressed? Ah, what a bother. Let me help you out of your clothes."

Anne opened her eyes wide and clutched the bedclothes to her in alarm. "No!" she screeched.

Lucy blinked at this reaction. "Of course I shall. How can you sleep in that uncomfortable gown?" she demanded.

Anne was acutely aware that Crewe was planted underneath her. "No, no. I shall change myself. I don't want to put you out." Then, desperately, she added, "It's so late."

"But I'm already up," Lucy said with damnable reasonableness. "And it will only take a moment." She spoke soothingly, as though she were talking to either a frightened child or a woman who had lost her wits. Anne had no doubt which one Lucy thought her. But she had not lost quite all her wits.

He had fallen at last into her toils! However, not wanting him to realize that she had been scheming for his downfall since she arrived in London, Anne tried quickly to think of a way for Lucy to discover him as a sneaking intruder. Finally she said, "All right. But—" she flung her arm, pointing "—will you help me search for my gloves first? I think I dropped them on the floor." Then, with wicked pleasure and as coolly as she could, she remarked, "They could even be under the bed." She struggled out of bed to help Lucy look for them, chuckling.

Lucy, being a model servant, began searching about without a word. But she was searching by the doorway, and Anne, eager for her triumph, became irritated and bent down and pointed under the bed. "No, Lucy," she said in an exasperated voice. "Here!" Suddenly, to her astonishment, she was yanked forward, so that she sprawled on the floor; her arm, almost pulled out of its socket, was held tightly by Crewe.

"I'll break your arm if you say one word," he breathed in her ear, squeezing her arm tightly.

Anne tried to pull away and yelped in pain. Lucy came running. "What is it?" she cried.

Anne couldn't believe she had been such a fool. She had no doubt he would break her arm, if he hadn't done so already. Furious, she said the first thing that came into her head. "I think I was bitten by a mouse!"

She wished she had never said it, for Lucy screeched with horror. "Oh, lawks. I'll get Reeth!" And before Anne could stop her, she scurried from the room. Anne yelped, "No, wait!" but to no avail.

Her arm was released, and Crewe emerged from underneath the bed. He was looking most disheveled, his hair rumpled and his face red with fury. "You are the wickedest woman!" he snapped at her, his eyes blazing.

She struggled to her feet, rubbing at her arm, no less disheveled and furious than he. "I wicked! What about you, my lord?" She blew her hair impatiently from her eyes and met his gaze squarely. "Of all the underhanded deeds. Trying to steal my diary!"

He opened his mouth to retaliate but caught himself up. "I haven't the time to brangle with you." His eyes narrowed. "I refuse to stay and argue only to be discovered alone with you in your bedroom by everyone in the house!" He stalked to the window. "Open, I see." He swung it wide and flung his leg over the sill. "Just as you said it would be," he shot back at her. Then, before her astonished gaze, he swung his other leg over the sill and disappeared.

CHAPTER EIGHT

THE MARQUESS OF CREWE shinnied down a convenient tree at Anne's window with all the ease and facility of a practiced libertine.

Anne stood rooted to the floor, like a regular gapeseed, staring at the window through which he had so dexterously disappeared. Damn the man!

She didn't turn around when her door was flung wide to admit a thoroughly ruffled Lucy, a ponderous Reeth ready to brave all little beasties and Lady Byrne, who had been aroused from her sleep by the bustle. This crowd created such a fuss and rumpus that it would have been gratifying indeed to Anne if the marquess had not just stolen safely away. As it was, her triumph had turned to ashes, and she was pardonably incensed by Reeth, who was beating about under her four-poster with a stick.

"Anne, Anne, whatever has been going on?" Lady Byrne demanded in a timorous voice. "Lucy said something about a mouse, which I couldn't possibly credit, but she insists it was. A mouse indeed. In my house? It wouldn't dare. I can't abide mice. Little sneaking creatures, always hiding in holes. Why don't they live out in the open? As though they had anything to fear. And of course, one is reduced to setting traps for them, and it's so lowering to have to set traps, don't you think? And they never seem to work, either."

Knowing too well the truth of this statement, Anne looked at Lady Byrne with a jaundiced eye but vouchsafed no answer, the only answer springing to her mind being so bitter an ejaculation as would have struck Lady Byrne into hysterics with shock. She noticed that Lady Byrne was attired in a dressing coat, beribboned in blue, and a lovely lace nightcap. Her aunt had probably just dropped off to sleep, and Anne felt compunction for having awakened her so precipitately.

"Oh, Aunt Honoria, I'm so sorry to have interrupted your night's sleep in this way. If Lucy—" and she gave this unfortunate a darkling glare "—hadn't rushed off in that madcap manner, you would still be asleep. Pray don't be alarmed. There's no mouse."

"No mouse?" gasped Lucy. "But, you said—"

"I was mistaken," Anne said with as much dignity as she could command, which was indeed a good bit and withered whatever speech was on the girl's tongue.

Lucy bent down and tugged at Reeth's coat. He peered up at her, a questioning expression on his face. "No mouse," Lucy informed him, shaking her head.

"No mouse?" he repeated blankly, shaking his head in a mirroring motion.

"Of course not," Lady Byrne averred self-righteously. "It's just as I've told you. No mouse would dare to live in my house. Of all the things to suggest. I take it in great offense, Reeth, that you would even think such a thing had occurred."

At this attack, Reeth was rendered speechless, laboring under a strong sense of ill-usage. He gave Lucy a look that boded no good for her, one that promised a good dressing down. Lucy held up her chin and sniffed. Lady Byrne seconded the sniff, but more loudly, and shooed Reeth out of the room with the words, "Really, Reeth, you must be in your dotage. Mice, of all things. And you crawling about under Lady Anne's bed. It's really not at all the thing."

He retreated hastily, and Lucy followed in his wake. Lady Byrne turned to Anne. "Of all the riots and rumpuses." She shook her head and gave a prodigious yawn. "It's quite ruined my composure," she declared, fighting to keep her eyes open. "I shall not manage to sleep a wink for the rest of the night." She yawned again and stared sleepily at Anne, who put a soothing hand on her shoulder and guided her out of the room.

"Don't be in such high fidgets, dear Aunt Honoria," Anne cooed. "It was all a piece of work about nothing. I daresay you will have forgotten all about it by the morning. Now, you go to sleep and pretend nothing has happened."

Lady Byrne yawned again. "But nothing has, has it?" She tried to open wide her eyes but failed. "That's what's so vexing. I don't mind being awakened in the middle of the night if there's something interesting occurring, though what of interest could be occurring in my house in the middle of the night I have no idea. Usually we're all asleep. But it's so lowering to have been awakened for nothing, after all. It has quite cut up my serenity," she complained, kissing Anne absently on the forehead, her mind on other things— bed, for instance. She promptly wandered into her room, ready to drop off into a blissful slumber.

Anne wished she could look forward to a good night's sleep. But she was so angry she could have pounded the wall with her fists. It had all come to nothing! It was lowering indeed. And to make matters worse, she had a headache. She grumbled darkly as she returned to her room and changed into her nightclothes. She was still grumbling when she finally climbed into bed and pulled the bedclothes up to her chin.

She had been so close to success. The Marquess had been right here. Right under this very bed. It would have created the scandal of the age if he had been discovered. Of all the underhanded deeds, sneaking into her bedchamber to try to steal her diary! The fact that she had been at great pains to tell him where she kept her diary and had played her Pantheon ploy with the hope of luring him into some outrageous action was beside the point, for he had behaved with unscrupulous iniquity by trying to make her drunk at his house this evening. Drunk enough so that she would be deep in a stertorous sleep, leaving him free to snatch her diary away at his pleasure. The fact that he had tricked her, instead of her tricking him, added fuel to her anger against him. For the marquess had not just tried to make her drunk. He had succeeded. How was she to know that three courses of food steeped in spirits would have such a drastic effect upon her constitution? It was most ungentlemanly of him to have subjected her to such a reprehensible menu.

And if that hadn't been iniquitous enough, she thought, fuming with outrage, he had taken advantage of her totty-headed state and kissed her!

She pressed her hands to her cheeks at the memory of that kiss, feeling a trifle warm. Yes, he had certainly kissed her. And what a kiss that had been. She felt again the quivering thrill at his touch. She reached out and snuffed the candle so that the room was shrouded in darkness. Why had he kissed her like that? she wondered. Certainly, he hadn't been deep in his cups himself. He would have taken pains to remain sober, considering his plans for the evening. It was a most uncharacteristic action, to say the least. And speaking of uncharacteristic actions, why had she kissed him back? She should have slapped him. But she had been incapable of movement, especially violent movement, so foxed she was.

As she drifted off to sleep she asked herself one more question. Why hadn't she announced to Lucy—and thus to the others—that Lord Crewe was hiding in her bedroom? She had let the moment pass and he had slipped away unseen. Was she getting softheaded about this arrogant man? She fell asleep more confused than ever, her last thoughts returning to the sweet kiss they had shared.

LUCY, WHO HAD herself endured an uncomfortable night wondering whether her mistress had become subject to distempered freaks, was obviously relieved the next morning to realize that her mistress had not been insane but in her cups. She clucked sympathetically and adjusted Anne's pillow so she could sit up comfortably.

The tray was placed gently on her lap, and Lucy went to open the draperies to let in the sunshine. Anne, however, begged her to refrain from doing so, the shrouded state of the room being more suited to her anguished state than light.

She was much revived by the hot chocolate and felt capable of braving the world in a surprisingly short time, but upon venturing down the stairs, she was dismayed to discover that Lady Byrne was entertaining morning visitors. When she heard the sound of voices she turned on her heel to make a desperate retreat, but Lady Byrne must have espied her, for she called out gaily, "Look, Anne, darling, we have Lord Wainfleet and Mr. Stanhope and Lord Sherringham here to pay us greetings."

Anne closed her eyes painfully but took a resolute breath and entered the room. She smiled weakly at the assembled gentlemen and asked them how they did.

"Very well indeed, very well indeed," Ninian averred. "Stanhope has been in high alt for the past week due to your kind offices, my lady, and so he came to express his gratitude."

Anne looked at him, waiting for him to express his gratitude. Mr. Stanhope reddened, then cast a desperate look at Ninian, who blinked and said, "Oh, but my lady, you realize I express the gratitude; he feels it."

Anne nodded in sudden and complete understanding. She made a halfhearted attempt to tease poor Mr. Stanhope. "Does Lord Wainfleet express the affection to Miss Farlow that you feel, Mr. Stanhope?"

Mr. Stanhope flushed hotly and shook his head. Ninian laughed out loud. Anne winced at the sharp sound and sank weakly into the nearest chair. Sherringham, who had been chatting idly with Lady Byrne, eyed her with languid interest.

"You look a trifle whey-faced, m'dear," he observed ungallantly.

Anne glanced at him askance before replying as stoutly as she could, "Oh, I'm just not feeling in high force, that's all."

Lady Byrne flew out of her chair and flitted to Anne, putting a hand to her forehead, her own face wrinkling with anxiety. "Oh, you poor dear. I had no idea. You look as sick as a cushion."

Such a description did little to raise Anne's declining spirits. She sighed heavily and gently pushed away Lady Byrne's hand. "No, Aunt Honoria. I'm quite healthy, I assure you. I simply did not get enough sleep last night."

Lady Byrne tilted her head, considering. "Well, I did not get enough sleep last night, either, and I don't look as out of curl as you do. But that's neither here nor there. I never look out of curl. It's a talent I have. I daresay it's because I never look exactly in curl."

Anne was spared the necessity of answering by Ninian, who cleared his throat. "Might I suggest that poor Lady Anne has become victim to the exigencies of a London Season? All this raking about at balls, assemblies and the like. It's most debilitating, I assure you. Perhaps she needs a diversion."

He turned to Mr. Stanhope for confirmation, and this gentleman nodded readily.

"What sort of diversion?" Lady Byrne asked doubtfully.

"Oh, I don't know," he began, in some confusion. Then he stopped and bent his mind to the problem. It took some effort, and he sat frowning for a few moments before he snapped his fingers and exclaimed, "I have the very thing."

Lady Byrne opened her eyes wide, and Anne tried to appear interested.

"You do?" Lady Byrne asked.

"Yes, I do," he declared, his eyes gleaming with triumph. "Vauxhall's"

"Vauxhall's?"

"Vauxhall's," he averred forcefully. "There's nothing like it. It'll put her in spirits in no time."

Lady Byrne was heard to protest that Vauxhall's could not be precisely considered restful, but no one paid any heed to this, least of all Anne. She had heard about Vauxhall's. It was a pleasure garden quite notorious for the goings-on in its environs. She perked up visibly. Her debacle of the previous night had been most dispiriting. But she had never been one to accept defeat with a philosophical shrug. As a matter of fact, she refused to accept defeat at all. Perhaps a night of rioting at Vauxhall's might offer an opportunity of ensnaring Pastor Max again! Her eyes kindled at the thought.

"Do you think Lord Denzil might be induced to accompany us?" she inquired in a dulcet voice.

Mr. Stanhope put up a protesting hand in revulsion, and Ninian eyed her with astonishment. "Invite Denzil?" he repeated, in a disgusted voice. "Don't you think that's going a trifle too far? You don't have to be that dedicated to—"

Anne stopped him with a significant glance at Lady Byrne. She wished to spare Mr. Stanhope's feelings, and she smiled most kindly at him. "I'm very dedicated to my purpose," she said, a trifle enigmatically.

Sherringham waved a heavy hand to an attendant footman, who hurried forward to help his lordship from his chair. Standing, the duke paused to smile thoughtfully at Anne. "I wonder if Lord Crewe will approve of this scheme of yours," he said.

Anne's eyes gleamed militantly. Denzil's requested presence was for Max's sole benefit. "I don't care a fig for his approval," she declared falsely.

His smile widened slowly, and he shook his head at her very slightly. "To be sure," he murmured. Then he sauntered slowly out of the room, supported by the footman's arm.

Anne was not left long in ignorance of Crewe's opinion of her scheme, for within the hour a runner delivered a message from him declaring his intention of joining her at Vauxhall's—no doubt in order to prevent her from embarking upon some scandalous escapade. Anne smiled to herself with a rising sense of pleasure, then frowned. She must keep in mind what she had set out to do to this gentleman.

Lady Byrne was as happy to hear of Crewe's intentions as Anne, for she could now cry off as Anne's chaperon. After the Pantheon Masquerade, she had no desire to frequent lively and questionable places. She could depend on Max to keep an eye on Anne, she declared, with more truth than she realized.

THAT EVENING, when Anne was preparing for her visit to Vauxhall's, she directed Lucy to lay out the red silk dress Madame Franchot had specially made for her. Anne was determined to do the place justice.

The dress was of a deceptively simple design and with a startlingly low décolletage. Anne fastened a ruby collar about her neck, which emphasized the expanse of exposed white bosom. She piled her hair high on her head, and Lucy placed some tall ostrich feathers in its curls. Gloves and a frivolous reticule finished her outfit.

Lady Byrne, upon seeing Anne descend the stairs, gave a scandalized gasp, her eyes starting. "What in the world do you mean by it, Anne?" she demanded in a failing voice.

Anne looked at her blandly. "What do I mean by what, Aunt Honoria?"

Lady Byrne pointed accusingly at Anne's gown. "That...that dress!" she gasped. "It makes you look like a, like a..." She couldn't go on.

Anne could. "Like a high-flyer? No doubt I shall fit right in. I've heard about Vauxhall's, auntie dear. I daresay no one will even notice me."

She was certainly noticed by Ninian and Mr. Stanhope, her designated escorts, upon their arrival at Byrne House. Mr. Stanhope was totally incapable of expressing his sentiments, but Ninian gave a long whistle. "What a rig-out. You'll put all the other women to the blush," he said enthusiastically.

Lady Byrne gave him a quelling look. "Anne's the one who should be in a blush," she said with feeling as she shooed them out the door, clucking disapprovingly. Anne could still hear her clucking as she was helped into the waiting carriage by Ninian, who climbed in after Mr. Stanhope. The door was shut, and the carriage was set in motion toward Vauxhall Gardens.

The gardens, occupying about twelve acres across the Thames from Westminster Abbey, was the oldest of London's pleasure gardens. It was, as Ninian promised, a most diverting place.

It was a fairyland park with thirty-seven thousand illuminated lamps disposed in different figures of suns, stars and constellations. Its spacious gardens were laid out in delightful walks and spotted with a wonderful assemblage of the most picturesque and striking pavilions, lodges, groves, grottoes, statues and paintings.

There was always music to be heard, such as a selection from Handel's *Water Music*, emitting from the great rotunda, as well as programs consisting of concerts of songs, sonatas and concerti lasting into the night.

It was not the aesthetic beauty of the place that made it so notorious, however. Vauxhall Gardens was a place of public amusement, open to all. Class distinctions did not apply. Ruffians, pimps and prostitutes on the one hand, and the haut ton on the other, made it both dangerous and glamorous. The combination was irresistible, and Anne, in her wicked red dress, looked forward to a very pleasurable evening indeed.

They arrived at the gardens to discover that Lord Crewe and Sherringham had already reserved a supper box. To her intense satisfaction, Lord Denzil was also seated in the supper box, as far away from Max as possible. Upon Anne's approach, he stood up and ogled her quite openly. Bethinking himself after a few moments, he retrieved his half-cocked mouth and waved his handkerchief in greeting.

Anne had the doubtful felicity of realizing that Lord Denzil was not the only man who was ogling her openly. She was the cynosure of all eyes. Her mouth closed firmly, and she held her head high but almost lost her composure when she found herself glared at with dislike by a bevy of painted, berouged women Anne had no difficulty identifying as true high-flyers. They obviously thought she was putting herself up in rivalry of their trade. Anne was much disconcerted by this incident but entered the supper box through the door in the back with a glittering smile upon her face.

Sherringham made a slight movement of his great girth as if to stand up to give polite greeting to Anne but obviously was content with taking the will for the deed and remained in his seat, smiling affably. Crewe rose punctiliously to his feet but looked far from affable. He took in her startling attire with an expression not only of distaste but also of deep disapprobation. He opened his mouth, no doubt to deliver some tyrannical order to the effect that she should march out of the supper box this instant and return home to put on something more decent, but he closed it firmly. Anne's eyes gleamed challengingly, and she was disappointed when he so effectively restrained himself as to give only a slight bow and then sat down again without uttering a single word.

She was much put out with him and therefore turned to Lord Denzil with a delight she would not otherwise have felt. Denzil hastened forward to lend his arm and place her in a chair next to himself. Anne perceived, from the lascivious expression on his face, that he had every intention of pigeonholing her for the entire evening. She humored him for some few minutes while dinner was ordered. Vauxhall's was famed for its roasted ham, which was sliced so wafer-thin that one could read a newspaper through it. Vauxhall's was also, and justly, famed for its rack punch. Several rounds were ordered for all.

Anne forced herself to laugh heartily at Denzil's fatuous witticisms and to slap his arm coquettishly while watching Lord Crewe out of the corner of her eye. Crewe's handsome countenance was marred by a deep scowl, and he was muttering under his breath. Anne redoubled her efforts with Lord Denzil.

He drank in her charms avidly, while also drinking the rack punch. He soon became quite flushed and inclined to lean a little too closely toward her. Anne averted her face and turned to Ninian, who was conversing with Lord Sherringham.

"This is a diverting place, Ninian. I congratulate you on your happy notion. I feel in fine spirits already."

"You're not the only one who seems to be in spirits," observed Ninian with a laugh in his voice. "And you, too, are to be congratulated," he said in a lowered voice. "You have him twisted round your thumb."

Lord Sherringham, who appeared to be on the edge of sleep, flickered his eyelids at this low remark and gave a smile. He glanced at Max, who was still frowning darkly and was beginning to make deep essays into his rack punch. "Indeed, my lady," he remarked, "you do seem to have him twisted round your thumb."

Anne was puzzled by the innuendo of this statement but was not given the opportunity to question him on it. Ninian suddenly called his attention to a beautiful woman who had caught his eye at another table. Anne decided to look about her as well, keeping her eyes determinedly away from Lord Crewe.

The gardens were well frequented this evening. The supper boxes in the crescent were filled with chattering, laughing merrymakers. A number of couples passed before their box, strolling languidly about. Gentlemen in military dress, ladies in silk gowns with spangled scarves placed negligently round their shoulders, Pinks, Beaux and Dashers all made the area rather lively.

A little too lively, actually. Anne froze with shock when one rather large, military-looking gentleman ran his eyes freely over her person. He was one of a number of men in regimentals, and he surveyed her with undisguised admiration. He even ventured to give her a huge wink. Anne almost gasped aloud. She jerked her eyes away, her face burning.

The large gentleman was most affronted by her snub, for he growled, "Hoity-toity, ain't you," before continuing on his way.

Anne was as angry as she could be, but she could only blame herself. If she dressed like a high-flyer, she must expect to be treated like one. She peeped from under her lashes to see if Crewe had observed the large gentleman's overtures, and her eyes widened in astonishment when she realized that Crewe was far from being able to observe anything. He had managed to down a surprising number of drinks in the short time since she had entered the supper box, and now there was before him a pyramid of empty glasses that was being expanded by the careful efforts of Geoffrey Stanhope. Pastor Max looked positively bright in the eye.

She assimilated this fact with mixed feelings. What could Max be about, drinking in this determined way? She turned to Ninian to demand of him his views on the matter, but Ninian was still engrossed in the beautiful bit o' muslin at the near table. He was whispering enthusiastically in Sherringham's ear, slapping him on the back and taking deep drafts from his glass. Sherringham was nodding periodically, but whether he was nodding off to sleep or merely agreeing with Ninian's raptures over the bit o' muslin, Anne could not tell.

Then Ninian's voice rose sufficiently that the girl sitting at the near table heard him. Anne saw her bite her lip and turn her shoulder. When she was rejoined by her swain, who had been chatting with some friend of his, she fell to whispering in his ear.

"No doubt about it," Ninian said now. "She's beyond compare."

Sherringham started to nod heavily but stopped and gave vent to a heartrending moan. His glass was empty. Of course, it was filled again.

"But who is that fellow with her?" Ninian asked loudly, squinting his bleary eyes and trying to focus his errant gaze on the bit o' muslin's swain. "He looks rather red in the face."

Sherringham made the effort of opening another eye to consider the swain carefully. After a long pause, he drawled wearily, "Perhaps he's a friend of our beauty."

Ninian shook his head violently. "No, no!" he shouted. "Look how red in the face he is. Why, I'll wager you the bounder is pestering our beauty, trying to get her to step out on a walk with him."

Sherringham carefully squinched his nose. "I do believe you are right." He sighed. "And I think she has snubbed him. Look how he smolders."

Anne covered her mouth to keep from laughing. It seemed that Crewe's unusual determination to drink heavily was catching.

"Well, I don't wish our beauty to be pestered by that bounder," Ninian cried out, referring disparagingly to the lady's swain.

"You don't?" Sherringham mustered an interested look. "What do you intend to do?"

"Expel him from the table." And he rose, swaying, to accomplish this task. Such an exertion was beyond what Sherringham could support without a pained shudder, but he made no protest. Anne, however, did try to stop him, but Ninian bore past her. She was forced to watch in horrified fascination. When the beleaguered bit o' muslin saw that Ninian, whom she obviously considered an odious monster, was about to swoop down upon her and her swain, she gave a sharp cry of terror and had little if any difficulty in convincing her companion of the efficacy of a hasty retreat.

By the time Ninian reached the table, it was empty. Anne saw him peer at it in total surprise. He blinked, then tottered back to Sherringham.

"Did you rescue our beauty?" Sherringham asked.

Ninian shook his head in wonder. "Couldn't." After a pause, he said, sighing, "She wasn't real. She was a dream."

Anne would have been highly diverted by this scene if she had not herself been as beleaguered as the poor bit o' muslin at the near table. Taking advantage of the fact that everyone was too deeply involved in his individual insanity to notice, Denzil put his arm around Anne's waist and started to kiss her neck. Anne tried to push him away, but he obviously thought she was merely being coy. When he pressed her foot significantly and tried to squeeze her thigh, she became desperate and turned to Lord Crewe, giving him a sudden shake. This gentleman came out of his trance and looked questioningly at Anne.

"Lord Crewe," she cried, "you promised to take me for a promenade through the gardens."

He stared at her intently for a long moment. Finally he said in a befuddled voice, "I did?"

"Yes, you did," she averred forcefully, pushing Denzil away again. "And I want you to fulfill your promise. Immediately."

He rose to his feet with surprising alacrity. "Of course I will keep my promise," he announced. "I always do the honorable thing."

Anne eyed him with disdain. She was certain he did. Still, being in his stuffy company was infinitely preferable to being in Denzil's, so she took his proffered and slightly wavering arm and supported him as they sauntered out of the box.

The cool night air seemed to sharpen his beclouded senses, and he said, without a trace of a slur, "Which path would you like to take, my lady?"

She smiled mischievously. "I've heard that Lovers' Walk is very pretty."

He looked into her sparkling eyes, his breathing suddenly suspended. He swallowed and said, "How appropriate."

They passed several colonnades and an occasional statue before turning into a pleasant grove festooned with lights. Crewe's steps became firmer, and he ceased to lean on her arm. He did not seem self-conscious at his unusual state, nor did he offer any explanations. Anne decided to be daring.

"I think you've been eating too many of your specially prepared dinners, my lord," she said.

His face swung to hers, arrested. "I beg your pardon?" he asked haughtily.

Anne gave a steely smile. "I succumbed to one of your dinners myself, my lord. What a pleasant sensation it is to be foxed, is it not? But I'm not quite used to it myself. For all my wicked ways, I rarely drink. Even deliberately.''

He could hardly miss the gist of her words. Yet he decided to skirt the main issue. "I'm not foxed," he declared. "I'm not even a trifle overtaken."

She gave him a look so eloquent of incredulity that he bit his lip. "If you're not foxed, my lord," she said with a dangerous glitter in her eyes, "then I'm not wicked."

He sneered and gave a mocking bow. "Ho, then. If that's the case, then I must be drunk as a wheelbarrow." He then ran his eyes over her far from demure costume and gave a sharp, almost bitter, laugh.

Anne stiffened, her eyes flashing. Fury boiled through her, surging up with such violence that she flung away from him in order to keep from tearing out his hair.

She stalked away, oblivious of her surroundings, so enraged was she, and she promptly collided with what felt like a wall. Her breath was knocked out of her, and she almost reeled from the impact, but two hands gripped her.

"Look what's dropped into my lap," exclaimed a boisterous voice above Anne's head. "You've decided to be a little more friendly, now, eh, my dear?"

She looked up to discover that she was in the grip of the very large military-looking fellow who had been so taken with her earlier in the evening. Before she could utter a single cry of protest, however, her arm was snatched by Lord Crewe. He snarled at Anne's accoster and incontinently dragged her away.

"I will not have you making up to any man while you're in my company!" he shouted at her.

Anne was in no position to defend herself, all her energies being spent on trying to keep up with Lord Crewe. She was not sorry to have been wrested so safely away, but her sigh of relief soon gave way to a gasp. The large gentleman and his regimental companions were following in hot pursuit, and they fell upon Max just as they reached the crescent.

"What," said the first man with whiskers and sideburns. "You keeping her all to yourself?"

Max gnashed his teeth at him, still stalking forward.

"Hold it, man," the bewhiskered brute continued. "Are you certain you're enough for her? Give her to us. We'll show her a better time than you."

Max swung on his heels, letting go of Anne's arm. He stormed back to the bewhiskered man and smashed him in the face with a flush hit.

"Oh, a set-to!" shouted one of his companions, and readied himself to lay in. Anne watched in paralyzed horror as he tried to pop Lord Crewe's cork, but to ill success. Lord Crewe floored him with a powerful right to the jaw.

There was a concerted shout, and the three remaining gentlemen leaped upon Max. There was a flurry of arms and legs as they crashed into the nearest supper box, overturning the table and breaking some lamps. Lord Crewe had embarked upon a scandalous Vauxhall affray!

A crowd gathered around the fighters, and Anne was jostled about. She didn't know what to do. She heard a familiar voice sound in her ear. It was Ninian, who was still puffing heavily from having dashed quickly to her side.

"What the devil is going on?" he exclaimed.

Words failing her, Anne could only point a finger at Lord Crewe, who at this moment was knocking two of his assailants' heads scientifically together so that they fell to the ground stunned.

Ninian flew toward him, pushing his way through the people. "My God!" he cried. "Max! Bethink yourself. It'll be all over town!"

Max paid him no heed and milled down another opponent. Ninian tried to render his assistance but was thrust summarily away by an interested viewer. Anne could hear bets being laid, most of them in Max's favor. And not without reason, for he was an unexpectedly able bruiser with a good deal of science and was never abroad. He ferociously assaulted the bewhiskered man who was just recovering from Max's first leveler.

As a few more tables and lamps were being smashed in the struggle, a number of waiters gathered to try to intervene. It was too incredible to believe. The Pastor Max in a Vauxhall affray.

She began to wonder how it would all end when a hand was placed on her shoulder, and she was swung around to face Lord Denzil. His eyes were glittering, and he was breathing most heavily. The air stank with the smell of spirits. "Come along, my little chick," he hissed in her ear. "This is our opportunity."

And with that, he clasped her arm in a viselike grip and dragged her as fast as he could toward one of the small summerhouses that dotted the grounds.

Anne resisted him as best she could. He put her quite out of patience. Enough was enough, she thought. If wearing a red dress had this terrifying effect on gentlemen, she swore she would never wear red again for as long as she lived.

When she found herself being pulled inexorably into a summerhouse, she had the presence of mind to give a cry for help. Denzil paid no heed to her struggles but thrust her forward so forcefully that her shoulder hit a wall.

He began kissing her face, and Anne pushed him away, feeling physically ill. She was certain she was going to faint when she was suddenly released. She opened her eyes to see Lord Denzil dangling before her. Crewe had him by the collar.

Without the least effort, Crewe carried him to the doorway, ignoring Denzil's swinging arms and legs, and threw him out.

Anne closed her eyes, shuddering with relief, and almost sank to the ground. Her descent was halted by Lord Crewe, who hauled her up by the shoulders and gave her a good shaking.

"What do you mean by it?" he demanded in a terse voice.

"Mean by wh-what?" she managed.

"You have gone your length, my girl," he snarled, his eyes burning, his face twisted with fury. "I won't have you sneaking off with Denzil right under my nose!"

"Sneaking off!" she gasped, outraged. "Why, I shouted for help." She tried to twist out of his hold, feeling justly exasperated. The evening had proved disastrous as far as she was concerned. It certainly was not pleasant being wicked, she decided.

"You didn't shout for help until you realized that Denzil was more than you could handle." He sneered at her. "If you insist upon leading men on, dear Anne, you must expect to face the consequences."

She started to exclaim that she had not led Denzil on but stopped when she realized that that was exactly what she had done. She fumed silently, and her hands itched to slap his face. "You are insufferable," she burst out.

He looked her up and down, his gaze making her feel suddenly hot. "Am I?" he asked in a queer voice. "Even so, perhaps you will suffer this from me."

And his mouth swooped down upon hers in a hard kiss. Anne's breath was taken away, and her head swam. Her hand lifted to push him away, but it fell back, and she leaned against him. His arms squeezed her so tightly that they felt like iron bands. Still she could not push him away. Her hand stole around his neck and pulled him more closely to her.

At the touch of her hand, Crewe gasped. He lifted his head to stare at her with smoldering eyes. "Am I insane?" he demanded in a furious voice.

Anne felt one of them must be, but she was too full of strange emotions to express this thought.

She didn't need to. Crewe glared at her accusingly. "You think to ensnare me as you did Denzil. You heartless bi—"

"Don't say it!" she stopped him, a hysterical note in her voice.

He ran a shaky hand through his hair. He gave a harsh laugh at her flushed countenance. His mouth twisted. "Well, I won't stay and dally with you any longer, my dear. I'll be wanted back at the crescent to give my name and direction for damages." He rubbed his chin reflectively. "And were there damages!" He gave an angry shake of his head as he stalked out the door. "There'll be the devil to pay for this night's work."

CHAPTER NINE

WHOEVER SAID success was sweet had been fair and far off indeed, thought Anne dejectedly as she listened to the expatiations of the ubiquitous Lady Jersey with as much interest as she could muster.

Lady Jersey was their first morning visitor, and she came armed with the tale of Max's doings at Vauxhall's. The Duchess of Byrne, who had not been favored with a recital of the night's doings from Anne, listened avidly to Lady Jersey's outpourings.

"Oh, it is on everyone's tongue, I vow," the woman declared. "It is beyond everything!"

Lady Byrne could not forbear casting a reproachful look at Anne. "Not on everyone's tongue," she said darkly.

Anne's gaze dropped guiltily. She could not sustain her aunt's disapprobation with equanimity. Actually, at this moment, she could not sustain anything with equanimity. She was feeling decidedly all on end. And she couldn't understand exactly why.

Lady Jersey continued with her narrative and went along swimmingly until Lady Byrne ejaculated, "You don't mean to tell me that Max was drunk!" The duchess was clearly astounded by this aspect of the tale. "Why, I find that vastly inconceivable!" she declared roundly. "I've never seen Max drunk. Not ever. He is the most abstemious creature. He has one glass at the utmost. And I think that incredibly forbearing because what's the use of drinking at all if you're going to have only one glass?'' she demanded reasonably.

"Well, Max had decidedly more than one glass last night," Lady Jersey averred. "He was as drunk as a lord, as the saying goes. Wasn't he, Anne?"

Anne nodded gloomily. Lady Byrne feebly clucked her tongue while Lady Jersey crowed with triumph. She took up her enthralling tale again with enthusiasm.

"And he actually took part in a mill?" Lady Byrne queried in a voice weak with surprise, interrupting Lady Jersey again.

"Yes, by all that's wonderful, he did," was the prompt reply. "It's the latest *on-dit*, you must know."

Anne made a wry face at that. The latest *on-dit*.

The duchess appeared undismayed, however. "I can imagine so," she exclaimed. "It is an incredible occurrence. I don't think anything in the Season can compare with it, do you? Not Lord Fenley riding his horse up the stairs at Lady Cork's or Lady Hammond dressing as a page and serving her guests refreshments. They're mere pranks compared to Max's escapade. Why, it is so out of character. Max in a Vauxhall affray! Whoever would have thought it?"

She lapsed into silence, so utterly moved was she by the incident. Anne was utterly moved by the incident, too, but not in the way she had expected.

This respectful silence was maintained for perhaps three seconds. "But then," Lady Byrne struck in suddenly with a frown, "if he was defending Anne's virtue, it's quite possible to believe. Max is exceedingly chivalrous, you know."

"Chivalry had nothing to do with it," Lady Jersey said flatly. "Quite five men were rendered unconscious by Lord Crewe's chivalry, as you call it. Lady Anne would never need to be protected from the attentions of five men at once!"

Lady Byrne took instant umbrage at this aspersion cast on Anne's charms. "Five?" she sniffed. "Paltry! I daresay Anne could be forced to fend off the attentions of scores of gentlemen, so beautiful is she."

Anne smiled weakly, trying to appear grateful for Lady Byrne's defense of her. But for some reason she did not really feel worthy of defense.

"But these weren't gentlemen," Lady Jersey pointed out. "They were military men. Quite beneath Max's notice. And he milled them down like a regular roaring-boy."

Lady Byrne shook her head in consternation. "Whoever would have thought it," she repeated, dazed.

Anne could endure this no longer. She begged, in a stifled voice, to be excused. "I'm not feeling at all well," she explained as she rose to her feet.

"It's no wonder," observed Lady Byrne. "To have seen Max in his cups must have been unsettling. It will take some time for you to recover. And then, to top all, to have seen Max engage in a bout of fisticuffs! Well, that's worse than anything. No lady of any sensibility could have endured it." She glowered at the subdued Anne. "Why you didn't tell me about all this the moment you came home last night, I'll never know." Although a lady of tender sensibilities would not wish to see a brawl, obviously she would love to hear about it.

"I did not feel up to it," Anne said feebly.

"And I'm glad she didn't feel up to it," Lady Jersey put in. "I do so love to talk scandals. And to announce scandals is an even greater treat."

Anne gave the woman a speaking look before tottering out of the room. Scandal. Oh, it was more than she could bear. She made straight for her sitting room and cast herself upon the couch, well on the way to falling into a deep fit of the dismals.

Of all the kick-ups. Who would have expected it? The fact that Max, so fastidious and so correct in all his doings, had actually succumbed to a bout of fisticuffs was conduct so extraordinary as to set the whole town on its ear.

So. Anne had accomplished her task. Done just what she had set out to do. She'd lured Max into a scandal, rendering him the odium of all eyes, and no doubt quite cut up his serenity. She should be in the whoops, not a victim of the bluest megrims.

She wondered why she was so undone by her success. Perhaps, she thought, it was because Max's capitulation had been so sudden and so completely unexpected. It was baffling in the extreme. She personally would never have expected him to behave as he had. And therein lay the rub.

She had come, slowly and grudgingly, to admire Max's upright character. He was above reproach, always to be depended upon to do the proper thing. To behave like a Pastor Max. The fact that he was Simon's brother had made his fine character all the more wonderful. He had been well on the way to restoring her faith and respect in the male sex.

He had been altogether a paragon of all virtues. Until last night. She reviewed the night at Vauxhall's frowningly, trying to discover what had brought on

Max's unexpected debauch. Max had been aloof but not austere. When she thought about it, he had been almost gloomy. Perhaps he had been gloomy at his failure to purloin her diary from beneath her pillow. Anne nodded with narrowed eyes. No doubt that was it. He had been looking forward to casting her out of London and had been cast into despondency instead at having failed to do so. Then he had relieved his frustrated emotions by drinking heavily and embarking upon a Vauxhall affray.

It served him right that he had made himself the subject of a scandal. Yes, it did. And she should be laughing herself into stitches about it. But her emotions were a strange mixture of bafflement, perturbation and regret, happiness and pleasure unaccountably escaping her.

Max had committed another action last night that puzzled her in the extreme. And she was not sure whether she regretted it or not. He had kissed her again. Quite violently. And she had kissed him back.

Why had he kissed her? Because he had been angry and drunk. But why had she kissed him? Because... Her expression softened. Because he had been so handsome, so strong, so irresistible. She stopped suddenly. She was being foolish beyond permission, she scolded herself. Pastor Max was not irresistible. Far from it. And why she should be indulging in these air-dreams, she had no idea.

She got resolutely to her feet and tugged the bell-pull. When Reeth entered the room, she directed him to order the groom to saddle a horse and be ready to accompany her for a ride through the park. She needed some exercise to clear her head.

Once in the park, she had not made great progress down Rotten Row, followed by her groom, who kept a respectful distance, before she was accosted by several fellow riders demanding to be told the details of Max's affray.

She found herself unable to supply them with anything beyond a shrug and a tiny laugh. The affair was of no consequence, she declared. A mere prank.

Claud Delabey Brown, riding a showy hack, was quick to contradict her. "My dear Lady Anne," he simpered. "Max doesn't indulge in mere pranks. In fact, he doesn't indulge in anything at all."

"To be sure." Anne smiled perfunctorily. "Perhaps the incident has been exaggerated beyond all proportion. I was there and found nothing that occurred to be of such profound note."

"That is because it pales into insignificance when compared to your own past escapades," a cold voice informed her.

She swung around in her saddle and found herself staring at Max, who was mounted on his black and looking impeccable in his buckskins and Hessian boots. The circle surrounding Anne suddenly cleared as if by magic, and she was left alone with him.

Anne felt her heart suddenly pound in her chest upon being so close to him, and she was certain her face had changed color. She surveyed him from beneath her lashes and discovered that he looked remarkably haughty and high in the instep. In fact, except for a certain pale tension in his face, he did not appear in the least bit chastened by his Vauxhall adventure. She assimilated this fact with mixed feelings.

"Well, Pastor Max," she said, after clearing her throat, "I'm surprised you dare show your face in public after your behavior last night."

His hands gripped the reins tightly, and his jaw clenched. Anne realized, suddenly, that he was exercising the greatest control over himself. "I imagine you think it a diverting matter that you've managed to make me the laughingstock of all London," he said finally, his eyes smoldering.

She sniffed and snapped, "Don't be so modest, my lord. You certainly lent me ample assistance." She put up her chin. "I didn't force you to drink so deeply, you know."

"Oh, didn't you?" he said darkly and somewhat mysteriously. "Well, that's neither here nor there. You certainly didn't help matters by dressing like a veritable trollop."

"What do you mean, 'like a veritable trollop'? According to you, that's exactly what I am!" she said hotly, her face suffused with color.

"Well, you haven't done much to dissuade me from that opinion. Have you?" he demanded. She peered at him in surprise. There was an odd note to his voice, almost as though he were pleading with her to give him a reason to change his mind.

She found her throat painfully constricted. "As far as I know, my lord, I didn't do much to *give* you that opinion," she said tightly.

He gave a bitter laugh at that. "That's rich. Ever since coming to London, you have behaved so outrageously that it has taken all my efforts to keep you in line."

"Oh, have I?" she gasped, her eyes flashing. "I have much to thank you for, no doubt."

"Indeed you do," he asseverated, his voice gaining force. "If it had not been for me, no doubt you would have committed some terrible folly that would have completely ruined your reputation!"

"And despite all your efforts," she said, a smile pinned to her lips, "I have succeeded in ruining yours, is that it?"

He looked down his nose at her. "My reputation could never be ruined," he assured her coldly.

His superior air goaded Anne beyond endurance. "Is that so, my lord? I'm relieved to hear it. Then I need not fear my victory rout being lamentably thin of company."

"Your what?" he demanded, jabbing the reins so that his horse tossed its head.

"My victory rout," she replied serenely. "A celebratory ball. You see, I feel I deserve some éclat for helping you finally to behave like a human being."

He looked at her strangely. "If acting like a drunken madman is your idea of being human, then you have certainly helped me to be that!"

She blinked, puzzled by the tone of his voice. "Well," she said reasonably, "no one else has succeeded in doing so."

His eyes gleamed disquietingly. "That is true. No one I have ever met in my entire life has had the effect on me that you do."

Her heart started beating violently, and she could only stare at him, experiencing an odd sensation of suspense.

To her intense chagrin, he laughed shortly, his lips curling. "And you think you deserve credit for this?" His voice was harsh.

"Credit and gratitude," she said lightly.

"It's mighty backward of me to be so undemonstrative, I know," he said sarcastically. "Perhaps Denzil makes up for my deficiency."

"You'll have the opportunity for seeing for yourself," she replied hotly. "For Denzil shall certainly number as one of the guests at my victory rout."

"You may be sure I shall be there, too, then," he almost shouted, looking as mad as fire. Then he jerked his reins and spurred his horse forward so that it almost leaped into a gallop as Max rode away.

She followed his retreating form with a pensive gaze. Well, she had had her victory over him, she thought to herself. Then she became quite still. But hadn't he had his victory over her, as well?

Lady Byrne was quite taken with Anne's notion of a victory rout. Indeed, Max's Vauxhall affray was so unusual an event as to warrant a commemorative ball. She entered into the plans and arrangements for it with enthusiasm.

"All the ton will want to attend," she declared, bending over a sheet of paper, conning an invitation list. "If only to see how Max looks after his escapade!"

And, indeed, acceptances immediately poured in. Anne, however, had no interest in any guest save Pastor Max.

ANNE AND LADY BYRNE were posted at the receiving line on the night of the ball. Anne was attired in a dress of white satin cut in a simple Grecian style. Gold thread ran through it, very delicately, and it was edged with delightful gold braid. A smooth gold necklace at her neck and gleaming gold armbands finished her costume, and she looked like a blond goddess. Or so

Ninian told her upon making his entrance, accompanied by Mr. Stanhope. They both looked in exuberant spirits; Stanhope seemed more incoherent than usual, and Ninian seemed bursting with news.

"He's done the thing!" Ninian declared without preamble in the entrance hallway. "He's signed up for a life sentence. He's to be leg-shackled. You can read all about it in *The Gazette* tomorrow, no doubt."

"In *The Gazette*?" Anne repeated, bewildered. Then comprehension sank in. "There's to be an announcement?" She turned to Mr. Stanhope, her hands held out. "Oh, how very happy I am for you. You've become engaged. I need not ask who is the lucky girl, need I?"

Stanhope, to her surprise, took her hands and pumped them enthusiastically. "No, you don't!" he exclaimed clearly. "And it's all due to you."

This unlooked-for eloquence caused Anne to gaze at him in wondering admiration. Well, they did say love made men do strange things.

"Tell me all about it," she urged. She fully expected Ninian to furnish her with the details, but no. Stanhope manfully related, "It was at Almack's! I popped the question, and she accepted."

"Oh, my." She waited expectantly for him to go on, but he obviously felt he had related all the salient facts. She sighed, her face beaming. "I'm very happy for you."

"Aye, and so you should be," Ninian put in. "The poor fellow thought he was all rolled up when Lord Denzil took a shine to her. But you rolled Denzil up, instead!"

"Oh, dear," Anne commented frowningly. "I daresay Denzil's nose must be frightfully out of joint."

The truth of her prognostication was soon borne out upon Denzil's entrance. If his nose was out of joint, he obviously had decided to drown his sorrows in Anne's blue eyes. For he attached himself to her quite assiduously, giving her a lingering greeting, bending over her outstretched hand for quite half a minute, and then attending her into the ballroom.

Music was already playing, and a number of couples had ventured onto the floor. Champagne was flowing, and all the guests seemed to be enjoying her victory rout immensely. But Anne doubted that she herself would enjoy it if Denzil remained so steadfast in his attentions.

She had invited him to her rout for the express purpose of throwing Max into a pucker. But now, regarding him with misgiving, and remembering his appalling behavior at Vauxhall's, she wished she had never invited him.

Lord Epworth provided a fortunate release for her this moment by stepping eagerly up to her and asking her hand for the waltz. She acquiesced gratefully, gliding onto the floor and mingling readily with the dancers.

Halfway through the set, she noted the entrance of Lord Crewe. A regular hum of excited voices started up as everyone caught sight of him. Anne bit her lip, not knowing whether to be annoyed or amused.

Lord Crewe seemed austerely oblivious that he was the main attraction. He looked magnificent in a dark emerald coat that emphasized his broad shoulders; a large emerald stickpin flashed in his snowy cravat. Anne took a deep breath. She had to give him credit. He certainly had an air.

At the end of the dance, she excused herself and hurried toward Crewe to give him her greeting. He had stationed himself beside a pillar where he was holding a desultory conversation with Sherringham, who was sprawling in a bergère chair. Within moments, they were joined by Ninian and Stanhope.

She held out her hand to Sherringham, who made the herculean effort of giving it a graceful kiss. She tipped her head coolly to Crewe, but he refused to rise to this bait; his face merely assuming an icy expression. Refusing to be discouraged, she smiled at Sherringham. "So tell me, Sherringham, are Max's doings at Vauxhall's a town byword?" She gave Crewe a fleeting glance to perceive the effect of her words. The effect was most gratifying, for he looked to be in the highest dudgeon.

Sherringham considered this question judiciously. "I believe there is a scandal brewing over Lady Sefton, who is flirting outrageously with a gentleman from a foreign embassy, but since she is always flirting with some gentleman or other, not much of a stir has as yet been created. Therefore, Max indeed holds the post of dishonor for this evening as the latest scandal."

"It'll have to take something pretty interesting to supplant Max's scandal, too," Ninian declared with simple pride. "I was never more surprised by anything in my life."

"Thank you, Ninian, for your vote of confidence," Crewe could not refrain from saying in a grave tone, which was belied by the gleam of amusement in his eye.

"Well, I'll always stand by your Vauxhall affray as the most interesting scandal of the Season," Ninian vowed.

This was more than Anne could bear, and a small chuckle escaped her. Crewe rounded upon her, outraged, but whatever scathing thing he was about to say was interrupted by Lord Sherringham, who cleared his throat.

"Let me take this opportunity, Lady Anne," he murmured in a deprecating voice, "to apologize for my reprehensible lapse by appearing in my cups before you at Vauxhall's. You must have been shocked."

"Not I," said Anne merrily. "I'm quite used to it. Simon was forever getting in his cu—" She broke off, biting her lip.

"Ah, yes," Sherringham observed smoothly. "I believe you did not approve of your late husband. Not surprising. I never liked him, either."

Max's head jerked at the word "either," his dark brows lowering, and Anne could only flush furiously and cast a look of burning reproach upon Sherringham. Sherringham looked profoundly unmoved. "Speaking of Simon puts me in the mood for a game of cards," he said imperturbably. "Simon was always one for gambling, wasn't he?"

Anne was spared a reply, which she was wholly incapable of making, by Sherringham's difficult struggle to his feet. All three gentlemen rendered him assistance.

Anne, rooted to the floor, watched the gentlemen as they retired to the card room. She considered following them, fearful of any other disclosures Sherringham might feel himself compelled to make, yet she felt so weak that she could hardly move.

The approach of Denzil, an intent look upon his face, gave her the impetus she required, and she hurried forward into the card room, Denzil following her close behind.

The gentlemen were already ensconced at a table, with glasses of port at hand. Crewe and Sherringham were engaged in a game of piquet, but Mr. Stanhope was lending Sherringham his assistance by holding and turning over his cards. Crewe pointedly ignored Anne's approach, merely downing a drink. Hoping to erase the impression of Sherringham's words, she took a deep breath and asked brightly, "May I join you?"

At that, Crewe gave her a withering look. "Of course you may not. We are gambling."

"Makes no odds." She shrugged. "I'm plump in the pocket and can afford to lose a few shillings."

"Absolutely not!" Max slammed his fist on the table so that his glass jumped, as did Anne. "It would be most improper."

"Makes no odds," she said, giving a dangerous smile.

"Obviously not!" he snarled, filling his glass again and draining it. He scowled at her, his mouth hard. "You positively relish committing improper acts, don't you. You're outrageous and wicked and not fit for decent society!"

Anne turned white as a tucker. She was rigid with pain, for the violence with which he expressed these sentiments hurt her more than she would have thought possible.

Wheeling around, she confronted Denzil, who was taking a deep draft of wine. "You wouldn't object to engaging in a bout of cards with me, would you? I would make it worth your while."

He gave a lascivious grin, his painted eyes hooding over. "What's the stakes?"

"My virtue, of course," she replied with perfect insouciance.

Ninian gave a bark of laughter. "If the wicked widow isn't at it again. What a hoax."

Her eyes glittered. "But I'm perfectly serious."

Mr. Stanhope audibly gasped. And Ninian cast an anxious glance from her to Lord Crewe, chewing his nether lip worriedly.

Crewe's hand tightened over his glass, becoming perfectly still. He seemed to swell with inrushed breath, and though he was keeping himself under rigid control, he looked on the verge of flying into a terrible passion.

Anne swallowed convulsively but stuck to her guns. "What do you say, Denzil? Interested?"

Crewe's eyes swung from Anne to Denzil, narrowed dangerously. His face was expressionless, but his stillness was unnerving.

Denzil cleared his throat and tugged at his cravat. "Interested? Why, of course I'm interested," he tittered, downing his glass of wine, an action copied by Lord Crewe. Denzil licked his lips and sniffed, looking quite bright in the eye.

"So you accept my challenge?" Anne prodded, her anger making her lost to all sense of reason.

The room was filled with a pregnant silence. All were tense with breathless suspense.

Denzil gasped then said, "Lord, yes!"

Max snapped. He threw his glass against the wall and then lunged at Denzil, his hands gripping the fellow's throat. "How dare you?" he ejaculated, squeezing Denzil's breath away so that his eyes popped. Ninian and Stanhope flew at Max, tugging furiously at his arms. Anne was too shocked to move. Sherringham also did not move, but not because he was shocked.

Max was pulled off Denzil, who was very red in the face and shaking with fury. He put his hand to his throat and coughed, glaring at Max with burning eyes. Taking a rattling breath, he sputtered, "That's the second time you've dared to lay violent hands on me, but you'll pay for it this time!"

"With relish," Max snapped.

"Name the place and time."

"Now. Right now!" Max shouted, too furious to listen to the shocked cluckings of Ninian and Stanhope. Several other gentlemen in the room who had been too fascinated by the turn of events to play at their cards set up a scandalized protest.

Denzil, who refused to sustain such an outrage to his wonderful person, complied icily with these terms. "Pistols?"

"Of course."

Anne blinked. It took a few seconds for her to comprehend what was occurring. "A duel?" she gasped.

"You can't be meaning to fight a duel in the middle of a ball!" Ninian almost shouted, shaking Max's shoulder.

Max swung on him. "Why not? According to the code of honor, it's the proper thing to do, isn't it?"

"Proper?" Ninian gasped. "It's mad!"

"Oh, go to the devil!" Max snapped, then turned to ring for the impassive Reeth, who was sent off for a brace of dueling pistols that had belonged to the late duke.

Word must have spread like wildfire, for a crowd of people suddenly surged into the room. Anne could hear murmuring expostulations and could see surprised and shocked faces, but she could not respond to them. She felt like ice. Her heart was in her throat, and she was shaking like a blancmange. She couldn't believe this was happening. It was incredible. And all because of her foolishness.

Max was removing his dark superfine coat. He tried to roll back the sleeves of his immaculate white shirt but was so well to live that he fumbled with them ineffectually. He swayed on his feet for a moment, then began pushing aside chairs and tables.

Good God! Max would be killed. He was obviously jug-bitten! "Something must be done!" Anne cried in a hysterical voice.

"Very true," said a calm voice at her elbow. She swung around. It was Sherringham, still seated comfortably at the card table. As Anne stared at him, her mind too frozen and numb with fear to function, he motioned languidly to Ninian. Ninian hesitated, still arguing with the deaf Max, then marched over to Sherringham and started to babble incoherently. Sherringham interrupted him, told him to hush and then took to whispering in Ninian's ear. Ninian's eyes widened, and he stared hard at Sherringham. "Do you think we ought to?" he asked after a tight pause.

"Of course," he replied simply. "It's no use remonstrating with them. They're both mad as fire and drunk to boot. Now, take this bottle and give one to Stanhope as well." He indicated two bottles of claret on the side table. "Don't waste an instant." His urgent words were belied by the comfortable tone in which they were uttered. Ninian took the indicated

bottles doubtfully, and Sherringham gave him a shove
of such surprising force that he stumbled toward
Stanhope.

Anne was stunned. They had to be all about in their
heads! "You can't be meaning to drink toasts at a time
like this!" she exclaimed. She rushed forward and
gripped Crewe by the arm. Reeth was reentering the
room with the pistols. "I never meant to go through
with the wager," she screamed in Crewe's ear. "You
can't duel. You might be hurt!"

He seemed totally oblivious to her words. She
looked frantically about her. The room was now
clearing fast, the guests obviously terrified of what
might ensue. There seemed to be no help for it. She
shook Max's arm, desperate. "Please don't duel," she
almost sobbed. "If you won't duel, I'll give you my
diary. Did you hear me? I'll give you my diary!"

Max turned abruptly and stared at her, arrested, and
his eyes seemed to pierce through her. Ninian, who
had crept up silently behind him, took this opportunity to crack Crewe over the head with his bottle of
claret. There was an explosion of glass. Crewe winced,
then sank slowly to the ground. Another explosion
was heard, and Anne turned in time to see Denzil top-
ple over in a heap while Stanhope wiped his hands with
satisfaction.

Immediately, there was a rustle of silk and the sound
of hurrying feet. Lady Byrne and a crowd of others
rushed into the room. "What was that noise?" she
demanded. "I couldn't credit it. A duel in my house?
Impossible! But that noise! It sounded just like pistols."

She suddenly espied Max's figure on the floor, the
red claret wine dripping from his head. "Blood!" she

shrieked, aghast. "He's dead!" And with that, she started to swoon away. Several gentlemen supported her.

Sherringham looked at them all and smiled. "Alas, no. Crewe is dead to the world, that is true. But if you'll use your olfactory sense, you'll realize the engine was not a pistol."

Lady Byrne recovered slightly and gave a timid sniff. Her nose wrinkled in distaste. "Wine!"

"Yes." Sherringham nodded. "The gentlemen settled their differences amicably over their drinks. Since their differences were rather violent, I'm afraid it required an entire bottle of claret. Each."

"They have settled their differences," Ninian struck in, "but I'm afraid the claret has settled them!"

There was a moment of stunned silence; then everyone in the room broke into gales of laughter.

CHAPTER TEN

ANNE RECOVERED FIRST, wiping the tears from her eyes. She shook her head, lapsed into laughter again, then gasped, "Good heavens, Sherringham, what a brilliant idea! I congratulate you on your presence of mind. It was first-rate." Sherringham acknowledged her praise with a very slight bow. She turned to Ninian and Stanhope. "And you! You're both pluck to the backbone."

Stanhope blushed, and Ninian waved a careless hand. "Thought it was my duty, thought it was my duty."

Anne looked at the inert Lord Crewe with a rueful smile on her face. What a picture he made lying unconscious on the floor in a pool of claret. She would never mistake him for a Pastor Max now.

Lady Byrne mustered all her energies and managed to direct the servants to herd the guests out of the house. Solicitous friends conveyed Denzil to his carriage, and Ninian and Stanhope carried Crewe to the nearest couch.

"Ought we to send for a physician?" Anne asked doubtfully, her brow wrinkling.

"No, no, my child," Sherringham tut-tutted. "It is a mere superficial wound. Cold compresses should suffice."

"Burnt feathers!" Lady Byrne was heard to gasp of a sudden as she sank into the nearest chair. "Pastilles. Sal volatile."

Anne looked at her, concerned. "Dear aunt, are those remedies quite suited to Crewe's condition?"

"Not for Max!" this lady replied with some asperity. "For myself! I'm certain I'm going to have a fit of the vapors!"

Anne hurriedly sent Reeth off for some restoratives, and soon Lady Byrne was provided with some smelling salts, which she sniffed at periodically while emitting faint moans.

Anne then turned to Max's reclining form. Her hand went out to smooth his dark hair. She had directed Reeth to apply a cold compress to the bump on Max's head, and Anne tenderly held it in place. My, but he looked handsome in repose. What a relief that he had not been seriously hurt. She could have kicked herself for causing such a rumpus. And she was profoundly thankful that no dire consequences had been incurred. What she had suspected when her early success had turned to ashes in her hands was now plain. She loved Max! Her heart sang with it. She had indeed made him human—all too human, in fact—but she had also lost her heart to him. All of her anger, her hurt pride, now mattered not a whit. Nothing or no one seemed to matter now to her save Max. She would gladly have given him her diary to prevent him from being hurt. She would gladly give him anything, for she loved him more than anything in the world. Her hand moved to his cheek, and she caressed it lightly, a loving smile on her face.

Suddenly, his eyes flew open, catching the expression there. He stared at her fixedly, giving a slight hiss from an inrush of breath.

Anne quickly moved her hand away, but Crewe caught hold of it and held it tightly. Anne felt a shock go through her at his touch and she quivered uncontrollably.

"You were going to give me your diary," he said softly. His eyes burned into hers, and she felt as though she were entirely alone with him.

"Yes, I was afraid you would be hurt, you see," she explained in stifled tones.

"And that mattered to you?"

"It mattered very much," she breathed.

He struggled to sit up, pulling her down beside him. He winced, and his hand went instinctively to his head. Obviously, he experienced a touch of a dizzy spell and was unable to hold his head up, for he was forced to lean his cheek gently against Anne's. She was unable to move but was heard to give a deep sigh.

"There's no need for you to give me your diary," Max murmured.

"No?" Her lips barely moved.

"No." His hand caressed her wrist. "Some things you said the night of my dinner party when you were in your cups forced me to think of Simon and to remember him as he was before he married you."

"And how was he?"

Crewe's mouth twisted. "He was spoiled. Willful. Always getting into scrapes. I remember father constantly disciplining him."

"And that's when you began to realize I wasn't a wicked trollop after all?" Anne asked in an interested tone, her eyebrows lifting.

He frowned, his face hard. "I should have given you the benefit of a doubt," he acceded finally. "As it was, I never even thought of doing so. You see," he said, with some difficulty, "it was easier for me to think badly of you than of my own brother." He gave a rather sheepish grin. "All from stupid pride."

Anne nodded slowly. "I thought it was rather stupid myself when I first met you." Her severe tone was belied by her smiling eyes. She surprised a laugh out of him, and his arm went gently about her waist, most probably because he needed support.

"So stupid," she continued determinedly, "that I vowed to teach you a lesson."

He looked at her with an arrested gaze. "A what?"

"A lesson," she repeated, smiling as sheepishly as he. "I decided to embroil you in some terrible scandal so you wouldn't be such a Pastor Max."

He became quite still. After a moment, his breath was released in a long sigh. "That explains so much that has been tormenting me," he said shakily. He looked at her closely, then put his hand compellingly on her shoulder. "Tell me," he commanded. "Was flirting with Denzil part of this reprehensible scheme of yours?"

"Ye-es." She bent her head.

"So you didn't care for him at all?" he demanded.

"Oh, no."

"You are incorrigible," he said in a grim tone.

She pulled at a button on his shirt. "I suppose I am." She gave an irrepressible chuckle. "But you must admit, I succeeded in my task. I embroiled you in a Vauxhall affray!"

"You certainly did. And don't forget that I got you drunk and climbed through your bedroom window. I behaved like a veritable rakehell."

She bit her lips. "So you did."

"You were just taking me down the primrose path!"

"So I was!" She peeped up at him, her eyes brimming with mischief, and they both burst into laughter.

"And now it's my turn to take you down the bridal path."

"I beg your pardon?"

He gave an embarrassed laugh. He put his hand under her chin and turned her face toward his, and Anne could see that there was a disquieting glow in his eyes. "That's a rather awkward way of asking you to marry me," he explained, his voice filled with barely suppressed emotion. "I succumbed to your wiles in more ways than one, my dear. I tried to resist you as best I could, but I found it impossible. You were just too fascinating. And when you flirted so outrageously with Lord Denzil, I was beside myself. I wanted to kill him, but I settled with trying to steal your diary so I could send you away from London and out of my sight."

"Were you disappointed when you failed?" she asked teasingly.

He pinched her wrist. "No, for it was the night of my dinner party that I was convinced you were a rare creature of spirit and quality. I knew that I loved you," he said with feeling, "but I was afraid that you had taken me into a confirmed dislike. When you offered me your diary, though, you gave me hope that I was wrong. Was I? Do you love me?" he asked in a compelling voice.

Anne's heart throbbed, and her eyes shone like a thousand lamps. "Yes."

"Enough to marry me?" His hand gripped hers hard.

Anne nodded her head, a deep happiness welling up within her, but before she could utter a word, they were surrounded by Ninian and Stanhope. Ninian let out a whoop of laughter and gave Anne a resounding kiss on the cheek. He them pumped Max's hand enthusiastically. Lady Byrne, who had long ago abandoned her smelling salts, fell upon Anne with rapturous sighs. Only Sherringham remained seated, smiling benignly.

"My dear Max," Ninian cried after the first excitement had subsided, "I do believe you've lost your head! I hope my hitting you with a claret bottle had nothing to do with it."

Crewe rubbed the bump on his head ruefully. "I do believe my senses are permanently impaired, Ninian."

Ninian, who had been joking, looked aghast. "Oh, I say. Not really!" he burst out. "But it was such a light tap."

"Not light." Max smiled down at Anne. "Never light."

Ninian sighed in relief and chuckled. "Oh, you're just shamming me." He turned gaily to Sherringham. "This is certainly a surprising event, isn't it?"

"Oh, no." Sherringham gave a delicate yawn. "They've been in love forever. I've known it for this age."

"Well, it certainly comes as a surprise to me." Ninian shook his head in utter amazement, as did also Stanhope and Lady Byrne. He surveyed Crewe, a smile in his eyes. "Pastor Max is going to marry the wicked widow." He grinned down at Anne. She twinkled up at him, well able to appreciate the exquisite humor of his point. "He certainly has given over his niffynaffy ways, eh, what?"

Max spared Anne from answering. He put his arm lovingly around her and said, "Yes, I do believe the wicked widow has reformed me." And then he fastened his lips to hers in a passionate kiss to show her his gratitude.

**For the millions who can't read
Give the Gift of Literacy**

One out of five adults in North America
cannot read or write well enough
to fill out a job application
or understand the directions on a bottle of medicine.

**You can change all this by joining the fight
against illiteracy.**

For more information write to:
Contact, Box 81826, Lincoln, Neb. 68501
In the United States, call toll free: 800-228-3225

**The only degree you need
is a degree of caring**

Take 4 best-selling love stories FREE
Plus get a FREE surprise gift!

Janet Dailey
Americana

A romantic tour of America with
Janet Dailey!

Enjoy two releases each month from this
collection of your favorite previously
published Janet Dailey titles, presented
alphabetically state by state.

Available NOW wherever paperback books
are sold.

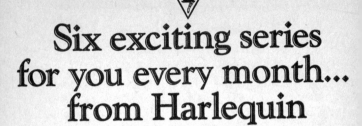

Six exciting series for you every month... from Harlequin

Harlequin Romance·
The series that started it all

Tender, captivating and heartwarming...
love stories that sweep you off to faraway places
and delight you with the magic of love.

♦

Harlequin Presents·
Powerful contemporary love
stories...as individual as the
women who read them

The No. 1 romance series...
exciting love stories for you, the woman of today...
a rare blend of passion and dramatic realism.

♦

Harlequin Superromance®
It's more than romance...
it's Harlequin Superromance

A sophisticated, contemporary romance-fiction
series, providing you with a longer,
more involving read...a richer mix of complex plots,
realism and adventure.

Harlequin
American Romance™
Harlequin celebrates the American woman...

...by offering you romance stories written about American women, by American women for American women. This series offers you contemporary romances uniquely North American in flavor and appeal.

◆

Harlequin Temptation ™
Passionate stories for today's woman

An exciting series of sensual, mature stories of love...dilemmas, choices, resolutions... all contemporary issues dealt with in a true-to-life fashion by some of your favorite authors.

◆

Harlequin Intrigue™
Because romance can be quite an adventure

Harlequin Intrigue, an innovative series that blends the romance you expect... with the unexpected. Each story has an added element of intrigue that provides a new twist to the Harlequin tradition of romance excellence.

Harlequin Books®

PROD-A-2

Enemies by birth, lovers by destiny!
Now in mass market size,
that richly authentic romance set during
the reign of the Roman Empire in Britain.

Lynn Bartlett

The beautiful daughter of a Roman merchant and a rebel
warrior of Britain must deny their opposing loyalties and
heritage when the ultimate passions of love become too
overwhelming to ignore.

Available in MAY or reserve your copy for April shipping by sending your name,
address, zip or postal code along with a check or money order for $5.70 (in-
cludes 75 cents for postage and handling) payable to Worldwide Library to:

In the U.S.

Worldwide Library
901 Fuhrmann Blvd.
Box 1325
Buffalo, NY 14269-1325

In Canada

Worldwide Library
P.O. Box 609
Fort Erie, Ontario
L2A 5X3

WORLDWIDE LIBRARY

DEF-1